TOO MUCH LOAFING AROUND

Sopwith knew instantly that his piece of bread, sliced insanely lengthwise, was an alien consciousness. Due to inadequacies in his upbringing, he erroneously identified its provenance as outer space, rather than the forty-seventh century, but he knew it was alive and he was pretty sure it was smart as a whip.

He waited, congealed with terror. The slice of bread opened one blue eye and looked at him, about to speak . . .

Other Avon Books by
Damien Broderick

THE BLACK GRAIL

STRIPED HOLES

DAMIEN BRODERICK

AVON BOOKS ◢ NEW YORK

AVON BOOKS
A division of
The Hearst Corporation
105 Madison Avenue
New York, New York 10016

Copyright © 1988 by Damien Broderick
Front cover illustration by Bryn Barnard
Published by arrangement with the author
Library of Congress Catalog Card Number: 88-91574
ISBN: 0-380-75377-4

First Avon Books Printing: November 1988

AVON TRADEMARK REG. U.S. PAT. OFF. AND IN OTHER COUNTRIES, MARCA REGISTRADA, HECHO EN U.S.A.

Printed in the U.S.A.

K-R 10 9 8 7 6 5 4 3 2 1

For
Robert Sheckley
and
John Sladek
who made me
laugh

STRIPED HOLES

chapter one

The time machine that materialized in the middle of the living room of Sopwith Hammil's rather nice bachelor apartment looked like a two-meter loaf of sliced bread.

As a trained television anchorman, Sopwith had no difficulty in estimating its size (unlike those luckless dupes who mistake distant re-entering Soviet Cosmos nuclear-powered spy satellites or flights of quail for fiery UFO mothercraft) because the time machine was jammed neatly into the sofa of his stitched leather suite, which he'd measured quite precisely with an engineer's metal spring-retracted tape only four months earlier in the exclusive Town & Country Shoppe.

The alien driving the time machine, and the machine itself, were wrapped in brightly printed wax paper, tamped over and glued at the ends.

The whole package looked just like one of the loaves of bread Sopwith had so enjoyed as a child, before the supermarket chains forced breadmakers to put their wares inside plastic bags.

Despite all the foul chemically active preservatives they inject into bread these days, as Sopwith knew to his cost, if you keep it more than forty-eight hours the inside of the bag starts to *sweat*, kick-starting the mold.

You can twist the end of a newly opened bag of bread. You can nub it shut with a plastic tie. You can put it in the refrigerator and hope for the best.

Next day you plunge your hand trustingly into the slimy plastic envelope, and find the filthy green fungus off and running halfway down the loaf. Before you've had a chance to eat more than three or four slices, the packet's a pulsing mass of indigestible flora.

Greenish white and ill-looking at the edges.

Nasty little spores, spreading and taking over.

You can empty the fridge and wash it out. You can scrub the trays, sponge them with vinegar and lemon. If you're desperate (and Sopwith often felt utterly desperate at this stage) you can rush to the supermarket and buy aerosols and powders, spray-ons and wipe-offs, each guaranteed to kill the insidious infestation.

It never works, of course.

Cockroaches won't inherit the world when human beings are gone, taking their cleaning agents with them.

Mold will. Purulent and festering, lurking and *sly*. Mark my words.

This loaf was not like that. Even as Sopwith watched it, agog, the top unzipped and a single slice of bread rose like some magical animation in a television commercial.

The slice of bread was crusty wholemeal, with a warm heavenly kibble odor.

The sight of it would have made Sopwith Hammil's mouth water if he hadn't already been stiff with terror.

He did not know the thing was an alien emerging from a time machine. Like everyone else in his culture he had been trained by what people ignorant of True Science Fiction Nomenclature called "sci fi" movies to expect aliens to emerge from *spaceships*.

Consequently, there was no doubt in Sopwith's mind that the thing jammed into his expensive crushed-leather sofa was not a loaf of bread but actually a spaceship from another world.

Even though he was wrong in detail, Sopwith was on the right track. This was hardly because he possessed piercing and unusual intelligence. Unkind critics of his national television current affairs program often intimated that Sopwith's intelligence was a commodity not in great demand. If his program had the highest Sunday night ratings in the country, it was probably due to his wonderful blue eyes, his muscular but deft physique, his voice like the thick, heavy liquid that rolls in endless waves at the hot core of the earth, and most of all to the devastatingly effective research background prepared for him by his gnomelike assistant Mariette Planck.

The reason Sopwith guessed that the alien device and its tempting crewperson was not a loaf of bread was because the aliens had made a typical dumb mistake.

The bread was sliced *lengthwise*.

I think we should pause here for a moment.

There's really little point in telling you any more about this singular occurrence *cold*.

Could Copernicus have discovered that the Earth goes around the sun if the ground (so to speak) had not first been explored by Galileo and his telescope?

Is it conceivable that Albert Einstein himself would have made that small step for a man but that mighty leap for mankind to the assertion that $E = mc^2$ if his way had not been cleared by the mathematical speculation of Henri Poincaré?

I tell you he could not, in either case, and in many others of similar kidney. And if you've never heard of some or all of these people, do please relax; you've just confirmed the necessity for a short but pithy lead-in.

For a start, you need to know that the sole reason the alien time travellers paid the slightest attention to Sopwith Hammil was a momentary glitch in the operation of their staggeringly powerful but overweening Symbiotic Computer.

This terrible machine was actually a hive mind made up of 10^{96} tadquarks, the smallest but nimblest life form known in that epoch. As you might guess, an organic machine of such complexity and speed gets bored quite a lot of the time, and as part of its research into the time knots tied around a series of Striped Holes (we'll get back to that), it had watched all the *Star Wars* movies ever made, all the Roger Corman movies ever made, all the science fiction and horror movies ever made, all the Spanish Main movies, both in black-and-white and in color, ever made, and indeed all the movies of any description ever made, even mini-series for television, even *The Thorn Birds*.

Later, it was to be alleged in its defense that it was precisely *because* the Symbiotic Mind had recently watched *The Thorn Birds* that its central processor became briefly unhinged and confused Sopwith Hammil with his fourth-degree cousin Mark Hamill, the swashbuckling but sensitive boyish hero of the *Star Wars* saga. It has to be admitted that they looked remarkably similar.

Sopwith, though, was no film star.

He would have been affronted by the comparison, and was, whenever it was drawn, as it was for a time before the word got around that he was affronted by it. He viewed himself as a media personality in his own right, and in fact in better than his own right.

Not only was his person admired by hundreds of thousands of sighing and swooning grandmothers, mothers, young women living more or less permanently but without benefit of clergy with young men, girls in puberty, and an entire cross section of the male gay community, but he was (so it seemed to Sopwith, and few people cared to tell him anything to the contrary) admired equally for his hard-hitting fearless interviews with the great and near-great, with the bosses of crime and the elected officers of the state, with Princes, Presidents, Prime Ministers, Popes, Potentates and, on sentimental holiday occasions, dear little aged polio victims with kittens.

As it happened, the interest of the alien in the time machine had been no less piqued on the evening in question by Sopwith's audience-warming aperitif.

You know how it works. While the big pre-program advertising teasers hit hard on some appalling item of political chicanery, or sexual corruption in orphanages, or drug abuse among media personalities on competing channels, you generally bounce on with one or two frothy soufflés. Get a grin on their faces and a song in their hearts. This time it was a five-minute burst from O'Flaherty Gribble, the astrological Renaissance Man.

Gribble was the perfect patsy.

"You have a Ph.D. in—how should I put this? in *poo* technology—"

The audience snickered in naughty delight.

"Dung recycling, yes, for energy conservation. Very important, you know."

"*Worm* poo, to be precise."

"We call it worm-cast ecoculture, actually, Sopwith."

Behind his thick glasses, O'Flaherty's eyes beamed with happiness. He loved being on television almost as much as Sopwith Hammil loved being on television. There was nothing self-aggrandizing in this pleasure, however. As a genuine twentieth-century Renaissance Person, the thaumaturge (we'll come back to that, too) felt it his ordained duty to reach the maximum number of his fellows with the latest word from as many of the sciences and meta-sciences as he could lay his eager little hands on. He possessed three doctorates, two diplomas (one, surprisingly enough, in surf lifesaving), and a licentiate.

"Hmm. You seem to have a thing for worms, O'Flaherty. Your first best-seller was a study of worm*holes*. Just let me get one thing clear," Sopwith said rapidly in his wry, deeply liquid voice, riding over the astrologer's muttered interjection, "are these the holes the worm travels through the poo in, or the holes the poo travels through the—"

His audience, blue-rinsed matrons and shaven-cheeked

chartered accountants, moussed girls and their louts, roared.

"Neither, you see. Different subject entirely. That's cosmology."

Sopwith turned a look of droll dismay into a waiting camera. "You're using worms to make *cosmetics?*" His eyes widened at the further implications. The audience were beside themselves. "No! You can't mean you're making cosmetics out of worm p—"

"Black holes and white holes in space," O'Flaherty shouted, relishing the sport. "But that was years ago. I'd prefer to talk about—"

"You're a Pisces, I believe, O'Flaherty. Is that what makes you the universal genius you are?"

"All nonsense, I'm afraid."

"You're not a genius?"

"Of course I'm a genius. No, those sun signs. Pisces, the rest of the constellations. Don't you want to hear about my marvelous discovery?"

"In a moment, O'Flaherty. The astrological signs are *non*sense? I'm shocked. How can the country's most famous astrologer say such a thing?"

"Well, it's true—for those of us living here in Australia."

Ah, yes. That startled you, I suppose. The thing is (and I realize you'll find this hard to take in) not everyone lives in London and Los Angeles, you see. Or even Birmingham, England, or Birmingham, Alabama. Sometimes a few quite important things happen in Dar es Salaam and Melbourne.

What comes to mind? Test tube babies, say.

That's in Melbourne, of course. In Dar es Salaam they make quite a lot of babies without any help from science.

Dar es Salaam, in case you're wondering, is the largest city in Tanzania. That's a country in Africa.

The National Museum in Dar es Salaam holds the skull of *Australopithecus boisei*, thought to be the skull of a pre-human living in Olduvai Gorge about one and three-quarter million years ago.

Admittedly, the experts in question at the National Museum in Dar es Salaam did not know that aliens in time machines roamed back and forth through history. If they had, they might have thought twice about the skull of *Australopithecus boisei*.

As it chanced, Sopwith Hammil and his guest were sitting not in Paris or New York, let alone Dar es Salaam, but in the austere studio of Channel 8 in the city of Melbourne in the State of Victoria in the Federal Commonwealth of Australia on the planet Earth, and neither of them felt himself to be hanging upside Down Under. In their funny old chauvinist way, they took it for granted that their hometown was the center of the universe.

Not that this was ever spelled out consciously. But it's what each of them thought. I suppose they did. Don't you?

In any case, as O'Flaherty Gribble was to learn within a few hours (somewhat to his discomfort), in thinking themselves at the center of the universe they were indisputably correct.

"Traditional astrology is based on northern hemisphere seasons, which have to be reversed here," O'Flaherty was explaining.

"But not the constellations, surely."

Gribble lurched excitedly in his seat. "Naturally not. But their *meaning* gets shifted forward six months, you see. It's the symbolism. How can December ice symbols work when it's a hundred in the shade?"

Sopwith glanced at the prompt that Mariette Planck had prepared for him. Good old reliable Mariette had it down to three bite-sized sentences. Smoothly, he said, "So a nebulous Australian Pisces, born in February like yourself, is really an intelligent, critical Virgo?"

"That's the idea, though you've neglected the precession of the equinoxes, which moves everything back one step. Actually I'm a Leo, with a bent for creativity."

"Gotcha. So astrology needs some of its cogs tightened." He glanced again at his prompter. Mariette had highlighted one point with a bright red box. "Tell us about the forthcoming Callisto Effect alignment. That should stir up some powerful influences in the ether."

Nobody had ever before seen Gribble flustered. It was doubly surprising, therefore, to find his face abruptly drained of color, his spine stiffened, his lips drawn back.

"Too soon to talk about that," the astrologer said in a voice like ground pepper rubbed into rare steak. Desperately he sought to change the subject. "Listen, my *big* news—"

Sopwith's nostrils dilated with the bloody scent, indistinct as it was, of the chase. He leaned forward tautly. "But haven't leading astrologers ridiculed your claims that the influence of Jupiter's moon Callisto will cause—"

"Striped holes!" O'Flaherty cried in a strangled voice. Sopwith frowned. The audience hung, breathless.

"Striped? You can't be serious. *Striped* holes?"

"Not black. Not white. Not even pink, like Hawking's. No, I've discovered a completely fresh class of gravitational anomalies." He licked his lips and forged on with a torrent of words and symbols nobody except himself could possibly understand, but everyone loved to hear. Striped holes. Dear God, Sopwith thought, checking with the clock. One and a half minutes to the commercial break. Let him run. This was science as sorcery, science as entertainment, science as weird mystery, strange and enchanting as a Druid's ancient runes. It was pure magic.

Sopwith was wrong. It was pure science.

In his home laboratory, O'Flaherty Gribble spent the

long hours of the day hunched over an IBM PC upgraded with an Orchid Technology PCTurbo 186 board. Using its own plug-in memory instead of the PC's random access memory, it freed up the built-in RAM for use as a blindingly fast RAM disk.

Perhaps I should explain that a RAM disk is a "virtual" disk that emulates an ordinary half-height floppy disk, but functions incredibly faster on I/O because all its operations are electronic, with no mechanical access until its contents are dumped to mass storage. Clear now?

Gribble in the privacy and safety of his own study made an entrancing picture.

Doffing his business suit and polished leather shoes, O'Flaherty favored a neck-to-toes sky blue robe embroidered in gold and crimson thread (by his sainted mother) with lovely ringed planets, five-pointed pentacles, Minkowski spacetime diagrams, hairy-tailed comets, frightening demons from the grimoires, angels with golden wings, engineering formulae often including i (the square root of minus one), a detailed map of Jerusalem in its heyday, and other arcana too mysterious to itemize. On his head he wore a tall conical wizard's cap topped with a merry tassel.

Despite this ludicrous apparel, or perhaps owing to it, O'Flaherty was privy to many deep and ghastly Truths. For starters, it had been the work of only a moment to unearth Sopwith Hammil's True Name.

While it is not the case that *everyone* has a True Name, it's fairly obvious, I hope, that no parents in their right mind could really call their newborn son "Sopwith."

Dwight, perhaps. Troy, believe it or not. Even Kermit. (Did you know there was a famous Kermit Roosevelt? Yes.) But "Sopwith" is beyond the bounds of probability, even in a universe containing time machines driven by a slice of bread cut lengthwise.

Mr. and Mrs. Hammil, in recognition of Sopwith's famous Greek billionaire great-uncle and oil magnate, had christened the child "Xylopod."

In Greek mythology, Xylopod was a famous king whose wooden leg had been driven at birth into a rose garden, where for the first twenty years of his life he served as a combined garden stake and scarecrow. Such servitude might have crippled a lesser man. Not so Xylopod. Using a form of isometric exercise taught him by a sojourning god with a taste for bondage and small boys, the lad's physical powers soon surpassed those of all but supernatural heroes of the stature of Heracles and Thermelware. Nor was his intellectual development neglected. Charmed by his handsome looks and the unremitting cheer with which he whistled witlessly even on the coldest nights and the rainiest Attic days, the beasts of the fields taught him all there is to know, including much lore lost to Man since our unhappy fall from the Age of Gold.

And so on.

It was a pretty story, and Mrs. Hammil (Pru to her friends) prevailed upon her spouse to grace their child with a name steeped in ancient Hellenic tradition and also giving maximum opportunity to suck up to their immensely rich but selfish and crazed distant relative.

In the event, old Xylopod married a fat opera singer and all his money was frittered away in ever more lavish and unbearable performances of Wagner's entire Ring Cycle.

You can see why young Xylopod exchanged his monicker as quickly as he might for a nickname of his own choosing.

You can also see from his choice how right the critics were in their estimate of his intelligence.

All this was made clear to O'Flaherty Gribble by numerological calculation. Who said a classical education carries no weight in an age of bar-codes, automatic library late-loan dunning systems, and Electronic Funds Transfer? In fact, he had used the same method to make his latest mind-wrenching discovery, the Striped Hole.

chapter two

By a strange coincidence, at exactly that moment just 197 years later, a mind-crackingly ugly woman named Hsia Shan-yun was all set to blow the crap out of the major personal records filing installation in the West Pacific Zone.

Exactly one moment after that, a monitor Bug put the arm on her.

As you must have noticed in your journey through life, be it long or short, rich or threadbare, estimates of physical comeliness vary quite a lot from place to place and epoch to epoch. So I suppose for an outside opinion you need a brief tally of Shan-yun's most objectionable and loathly features, as registered by the people of her time and zone:

She was a horrifyingly tall Valkyrie, just under two meters from her size-ten track shoes to the top of her wildly flowing black mane.

Eyes of slashing jade green glared out at the world she despised under slanting, Oriental eyelids.

Her mouth was ripe and full, hardly the neat, demure pallid line esteemed by leading fashion experts of the late twenty-second century.

I won't even talk about her breasts, or the violent animal swing of her muscular body, or the way her legs stretched most of the way from earth to sky and her arms seemed fitted by evolution to a role quite other than punching data into a terminal fifteen hours a day. A detailed list would be disgracefully sexist, whether by our standards or hers.

Take it from me. Hsia Shan-yun was a pig.

Her benighted parents, the world's last Confucian Scientologists, had hidden her in a small shielded bottle during the Reconstruction Phase, when genetic engineers in geosynchronous orbit had broadcast whole-body altering messages to the gonads of the entire planet. In consequence, the unfortunate creature looked like an abominable throwback to that peak epoch of nutrition-driven Brute Expressionism— the twentieth century.

Naturally, Shan-yun compensated for her atrocious looks by denial and fantasy. Day and night she read forbidden books (all books, of course, being forbidden, but some being incredibly more forbidden than others, and it was this kind she crammed into her perverted brain).

The books she sought high and low were about the twentieth century, that sink of degradation and physical excess.

Best of all, she loved books about inner-city funrunning.

In the depths of the empty municipal sewers, during darkest night, aided only by the light from her Watchplate tuned to an empty channel, she pounded out the klicks in her handmade track shoes, until inhumanly shaped muscles swelled in her legs.

Next of all she loved books about working out with weights.

Staring with a swollen heart at flat photographs of Bev Francis and Arnold Schwarzenegger, she hack-squatted and bench-pressed, chest-flyed and lat-extended, leg-lifted and bicep-curled. What this did to her already distorted atavistic frame can only be left to the imagination, because I really couldn't stand the aggravation.

How did the robot Bugs know what Shan-yun had been up to? She'd taken every precaution. The whole thing had been planned out in exquisite detail for nearly fifteen months. She'd gone over every single detail of the operation a dozen times, from the initial routine of getting a job in Pacific Data Central to the final step of smuggling her home-plaited Striped Hole into the terminal terminal.

She hadn't been able to find a flaw in the plan but obviously there'd been a flaw you could drive a Bug through.

The robot cop rolled up beside Shan-yun just as she was entering the Personal Information Bubble Banks, as she had every right to do, being assistant trainee data slibber.

She watched it coming at her from the corner of her slitted, tilted, jade-glowing eyes and kept walking.

Even though she was by now very, very good at running, running would not have helped, as it turned out.

A cloud of gossamer filaments belched from the Bug's chest spigots and settled on her like acid rain.

"Shit!" cried Hsia Shan-yun, proving yet again that she was an evil lowlife throwback.

Tiny itching threads coated her from head to foot, leaving uncovered only her eyes, ears and nostrils. Achieving that effect had consumed a decade of nonstop dedicated research in the National Goo Laboratories, but Hsia Shan-yun was not impressed. She hissed with rage. She spat. There wasn't much else she could do, because the filaments put their tiny hands together and squeezed, tightening into a body-hugging plastic shell. Just enough slack was left around Shan-yun's hideously overdeveloped rib cage and chest for her to breathe, but only just enough.

She started to fall flat on her face.

Before the statuelike form she now was could topple to the tiles and shatter, the monitor Bug whipped out metal tentacles and nestled her carefully against its own hard torso.

"Citizen Hsia," the thing intoned, "it is my unhappy duty to take you into protective custody, for both your own highest good and that of the republic."

"Mmmnbbn," Shan-yun explained. "Gmmngb."

"I regret the temporary restraint on your freedom of

speech," the tin cop said unctuously, "but rest assured
you will be permitted full range of expression as soon as
we arrive at Medical Six. And how," it added with a low
chuckle, and spun about, accelerating out of the Bubble
Bank.

"We intend to indict you for conspiracy against the
State," it re-added for good measure. "Appropriate re-
medial steps will follow forthwith. Oh my, yes."

Did this unwelcome mechanical badinage affect the ap-
prehended criminal?

What do *you* think?

Shan-yun was rather miffed.

No, that doesn't quite capture it. She was seriously
alarmed at her prospects.

Actually, she was in a turmoil of panic.

Not to put too fine a point on it, she was ready to shit
herself.

The monitor Bug rolled swiftly though the foyer of Data
Central with Shan's rigid torso tucked against it like a
huge ungainly swaddled baby, except that they didn't deal
that way with babies anymore.

When her head happened to tilt that way, Shan-yun had
no difficulty in seeing people scurrying out of the way.
The chief slibber, coming in from a lunch of chives, peat-
growth, and yoghurt sausages, blenched and turned aside
without a word.

"Fairweather friend," Shan tried to shout bitterly, but
it came out as another collection of vowelless unpalatal-
ized consonants.

Outside the building, machine and captive swung down
a ramp to a thoroughfare marked MEDICAL ONLY.

In 197 years time, that's a sign to make your blood run
cold. Well, I suppose it is already, to be brutally frank.

The monitor jacked without hesitation into a high-speed
conveyor unit, thoughtfully raising a shield to keep the
wind out of Shan's eyes.

The harsh violet lights of the tunnel went blurry with

speed. Shan-yun's tummy tried to sneak away, but her backbone wouldn't let it. Half a minute later it got its revenge.

"All still in one piece, I hope, dear?" the machine said in Shan's reeling ear. "Here we are. Have a nice day, now."

The monitor coasted into the aseptic whiteness of a medical bay. You can always tell, 197 years from now, when you've reached a medical bay. The atmosphere reeks of such a high-toned blend of purity and righteousness you want to throw up.

Two crisp blue-garbed apes stepped out of a lift. Mental health and social adjustment radiated from their every pore.

"Citizen Hsia!" cried the one on the right. "Welcome to Medical Six." His demeanor blended professional cheeriness with personal stoic resignation to the iniquity of social deviants with Striped Holes tucked inside smelly parts of their bodies.

"Kindly place the citizen on the couch and return to your post," said the one on the left. Still locked solid in her plastic cocoon, Shan-yun was positioned carefully on a form-fitting cot. The Bug rolled away whence it had come without a word of farewell.

The mind-crackingly ugly woman stared up at her doctors and tried to set off the Hole. Nothing happened. Her fingers would not bend. The muscles in her belly spasmed but she lay motionless. The Hole spun uselessly inside her, quite beyond her control.

"Well, Ms. Hsia," the first ape told her, "you've certainly got yourself into a peck of trouble."

"Yep. No untruth there. Let's hope for your sake we can straighten you out, ethics-wise, without having to reduce you to a veggie."

Under the plastic skin, cold sweat jumped from Shan's forehead in almost exactly the way moisture develops on the inside of a loaf of plastic-wrapped bread. It was a disgusting and depressing sensation.

"Brainscrub," one of the creatures said reflectively. "If you can't use it, you just gotta lose it."

"It's a tragedy, though, Frank, She's a person of evident resource. How many of us could plait a Striped Hole without being picked up at the nudge-horizon stage? That's skill, Frank, whether or not we care to admit it. Talent."

"Yet we mustn't forget that she's abused her abilities to the detriment of the State."

"I'd never let that slip my mind, Frank, but it seems our fellow citizen must have done so." He peered down into Shan's eyes with a look of loathing and concern. Shan's eyes by now were brimming to overflow with tears of fury and terror. In fact, Shan's eyes took the opportunity to try to leap from her head and tear the ape's sanctimonious tongue from his head, but being organs ill adapted by evolution to that function, they had to content themselves with bulging in red-shot hatred.

"You should have recognized your own sickness," Frank told her. "You ought to have boldly stepped forward for voluntary treatment."

The threads of the cocoon tightened and the ape shook his head ruefully.

"Relax, Ms. Hsia. Anger is a wasteful and antisocial emotion. A good case has been made for the view that all emotion is wasteful and antisocial, but I don't subscribe to that view. Live and let live, I say."

A colorful board of indicators flashed and chimed. Shan-yun seethed.

"We'll be sending you through to the Analyst any moment now, Ms. Hsia, and I've got to tell you, it won't look good on your record if you're harboring resentment."

A muffled series of explosive noises came from the cocoon.

A melodious tone sounded from the lift.

"Ah, there we are now. No need for anxiety, Ms. Hsia. Truly. You'll go straight through for analysis and judgment as soon as the techs have removed the cocoon and that Striped Hole you inserted into yourself."

The other ape nodded vigorously, leaning across Shan-yun with an aerosol can. "Absolutely correct. Remember—our job is to get you *well*." He squirted spray into her nostrils. The room tilted and banged the side of her head.

She was not quite unconscious as the apes began to push the couch and her numb body into the lift. "Candidly, Ted," she heard Frank say, as the darkness ripped her mind into silly small shreds, "these deviants give me the gol-durned *creeps*."

chapter three

In the monitor, set at an angle into Sopwith's desk, the Minister's pudgy face was white as scone-mix and sprinkled with nasty droplets.

Sopwith flicked his gaze back to the living man, across the desk from him in the studio. The fellow's ghastly shifty eyes scuttled away. Camera 2 moved in. In the monitor, 2's close-up turned him into a frightened corpse.

Sopwith's body hummed with the animal electricity of the hunt, and so did his audience. He shot them a quick glance. They sat tense and joyful on their uncomfortable vinyl and tubular metal bleachers, waiting for him to kill.

If this had been the Roman Empire they'd have been shouting for blood. Every thumb down.

Any last trace of levity left over from O'Flaherty Gribble's earlier fun & games had evaporated as completely as a spatter of piss in the hot radiating core of a nuclear reactor, which was what Sopwith meant his audience to think the Minister thought they were worth, and in fact what he wanted them to think they would probably *become* the day the Minister got his uranium bill through.

Bloody politicians, Sopwith thought with contempt. They never learn, except the ones who pay for media advice, and even they disregard it half the time.

This idiot had refused to get his face powdered and made-up before the interview. Effeminate, he said, waving the girl away. He was paying the price now.

Camera 1's red light went on, and Mariette's prompter shot a small lump of barbed information into Sopwith's field of view. On the monitor, his own features replaced the Minister's. His jaw hardened, a dramatic sight.

"In fact, Minister, we're talking about the multinational whose reactor melted down last week in Pakistan."

Harcourt, the corporation's PR man, tried to head the politician off with his own interruption. He didn't stand a chance.

"The same company that made your wife's trust a gift of 5,000 shares a little over a year ago," Sopwith added murderously.

Up in his eyrie, the director knew exactly what was afoot and gestured to the sound man, whose fingers glided over the broad array of toggles like a concert pianist's. Harcourt's mike cut off as Sopwith's voice rose in cruel indignation. The man's careful rebuttal came through the other mikes as an intrusive mutter.

"A gift, Minister," Sopwith said in a more relaxed tone, "made just six months before your . . . interesting . . . reversal of policy on the protection of Aboriginal sacred sites."

Camera 2 stayed on the appalled politician, moved in like a glassy-eyed Cyclops to peer into his nostrils, probe his dental work, check out the scurfy dandruff in the bushy line of his run-down but aristocratic eyebrows.

A bubble of mad rage burst inside the Minister's brain.

There's only so much you can put up with, even when your career hangs upon projecting your lofty indifference to the unsubstantiated ravings of lower-class rubbish like Sopwith Hammil.

If Camera 2 had been able to get right inside his ear and track through his brain to the Thought Center, it would have found it momentarily unattended.

Cold lonely winds piped through its open doors. Cakes and tea cooled on the long polished table, crumbs were scattered on the dear little lace doilies. Linen napkins lay on the parquet flooring. Chairs had been thrown back heedlessly, the whiskey decanter left unstoppered.

The Minister had gone out for the day.

His eye went bloody as all the neurochemicals in his back lobes began to froth and boil and turn the colors chemicals go when you burn them with a Bunsen flame inside a dirty test tube.

A gargling noise climbed through his internal pipes, picking up foul dyspeptic odors as it came, and belched from his mouth in a roar of unseemly emotion.

"I won't have these insinuations, you rancid little guttersnipe!"

It would not be rash to surmise that the Minister had lost a measure of his normally impeccable self-control.

"I won't submit to a witch-hunt!"

He did not quite climb onto his chair and bang his forehead on the heavy lights blaring down into his maddened face.

"Television stations in other countries have lost their licenses for less than this, by George! Do you really believe you can—"

Sopwith kept his face expressionless, let the picture in the monitor linger one last destroying moment longer than was humanly decent.

Finally he raised his right index finger and scratched his ear lobe.

His producer took the cue, cut to Harcourt.

In the middle of a sentence, the PR man's sound came back up. Sopwith left him no chance to clarify the half-truth about the uranium shares. The clock showed twenty seconds to the end of the program. As always, he'd timed the blow-off perfectly.

I suppose you think it's easy, getting people to drop their trousers in public like that.

It's not easy, take it from me. You only think it is because you're used to watching prerecorded stuff. "Sixty Minutes," all that great hard-hitting investigative report-

age safely in the can days ahead of air, ready for trimming
and splicing and orchestrating and checking with the law-
yers.

Sopwith did it cold and made it hot, and because it went
out live no one could stop him once it was done.

Closing was a piece of cake.

As the canned applause and theme music rolled with
the credits, the floor manager, deft master of diplomacy,
led the reeling and expostulating Minister away adroitly in
the direction of the watering trough. The PR man thought
to linger, changed his mind, chased after them.

Sopwith stretched. His armpits were wet with well-
earned perspiration and sweet with his expensive deodorant and men's fragrance. He glanced around. The
auditorium was emptying noisily. O'Flaherty Gribble was
nowhere to be seen. Must have gone early without a drink.
No, bugger doesn't drink.

Nodding to his grinning staff, Sopwith made straight for
his office.

The program had been rougher than usual. Not to mince
words, it had been *filthy*.

By and large, Sopwith could come near to flaying a
victim and then retrieve him, shake hands after the blow-
off, grinning like a star whose presence makes everyone
else a star too, reassure the fellow, and somehow, myste-
riously, against all sense, lay up a store of favor, and all
this with his victim hardly aware that he'd been bought by
the fiend who minutes earlier had held his roasting arse
over the flames.

You can't always be a pussycat, Sopwith told himself,
opening the door to his office.

Every now and then it's necessary to go the whole hog.

Cement your reputation as the public's watchdog. Sopwith Hammil, feared by the mighty, loved by the common
folk. Crusader, bon vivant, a man seen in the right places
but only at his own choice.

It made Sopwith quite giddy to think about how wonderful he was.

"Sopwith, you were wonderful!"

He raised his head sharply at Mariette Planck's eager voice, and forced himself with a mental crowbar to smile at the gnomish young woman.

Actually she wasn't gnomish. Mariette was just very, very unattractive. By Sopwith's late twentieth-century beef-fed high-adrenaline standards, she was unattractive in precisely the way Hsia Shan-yun wasn't.

If Sopwith Hammil had clapped eyes on Hsia Shan-yun, the most dreadfully ugly female of her species in the century of her birth, he would have fallen to the ground in a fit of lust and depression.

Even up-and-coming media superstars in Melbourne, Australia, do not aspire to the likes of Hsia Shan-yun, not even at the close of the twentieth century.

Bianca Turner, maybe, with a good wind at your back. Tina Jagger, given your best shot. Madonna? Who cares.

Hsia Shan-yun, in terms of late twentieth-century film and television culture a Goddess beyond compare (except for her furious intelligence and forthright self-determination which would certainly stand in her path), Hsia Shan-yun is plainly out of the question for the likes of Sopwith Hammil.

Mariette Planck, by contrast, gazed up at her boss with the worshipful devotion the owner of a German short-haired pointer wishes hopelessly it would direct at the owner of a German short-haired pointer, though the great handsome long-eared fools never do, being far too distracted by the need to tear holes in the velvet sofa and bury empty dog-food cans there.

As we have seen, Sopwith was a child of his times. A child, indeed, behind his times. He was a careerist and an unashamed male chauvinist.

He could hide this detestable trait well enough when obliged to chat up fellow lady television presenters, women

astronauts, and female bodybuilders like Bev Francis of
Melbourne, Australia, but in his heart of hearts (a crude,
smirking and sniggering schoolboy of an organ) he thought
women were good for three things only, all German and
all starting with the letter *K*.

He was not, however, in favor of marriage.

Sopwith had been saved by abortionists and the Pill from
the fate of an ancient lineage of tumblers, mountebanks,
stage actors, movie comedians, and the rest of his trade—
saved, that is, from being shotgunned into wedlock as a
result of his own feckless fertile fooling around.

Twenty, fifteen years earlier, it would have been man-
datory for a media superstar on the rise to be married,
unless he were English and on the make (and as anyone
could see there were sound eugenic reasons for being glad
that media superstars of that kind kept their genes out of
circulation).

Twenty, fifteen years in the future, it is going to be
absolutely *essential* for television pundits and anyone else
in the public eye to be married, following the Great Combined Anthrax Jihad and Creation Science Crusade, because the ayatollahs and mullahs and Right to Life pastors
are going to come around every morning to check your
sheets, and if they find a little stain there and you a man
not married at least once in the village mosque they are
going to have you hauled into the middle of the town square
and make everyone jeer at you for a short time before they
amputate and burn the offending anatomical implements.
If you're a *woman* not married in these circumstances
(hardly likely, given the paucity of women TV pundits in
that time frame), you'll just be stoned to death and be
done with it.

I shouldn't have told you that. It's wrong to know how
the future will come out. Tends to sap the will, don't you
find?

The point to recall, however, is this:

Just at the moment we're recounting, Sopwith in his

swinish way believes he has every reason to remain a bachelor.

If he remains a bachelor, he can continue unchecked to enjoy the disgraceful fruits of that estate, which he now does every chance he gets, which, looking and sounding the way he does, and despite the gains of the Women's Movement, is most of the time.

He doesn't simply enjoy the fruits.

Sopwith chews up the flesh of the fruits, and then he chews up the skin, and then he eats and swallows the core, before he spits out the pits.

He had never spat Mariette Planck's pits out because, by Sopwith's shameful sexist standards, Mariette Planck was the pits to begin with.

Those ankles! They could have supported a fairly sturdy bank building, but the legs would not have held it far enough off the ground to satisfy the council building inspectors.

The face on her! Like an exploded pumpkin.

Muddy little squinty eyes.

Hair on top filched from the innards of some Italian family couch sat on by spaghetti-fed buttocks for fifty years and then left outside in the rain when they got a lovely new round-the-corner sofa carved with angels and bowls of grapes and the Virgin Mary and Saint Veronica holding her bloody towel and caryatids with pointed tits from Franco Cozzo the furniture king with stores in Footersgray and Brunerzwick. I realize some of this will mystify you unless you live in Melbourne, Australia, and watch a lot of late-night television, but live and let's live, okay? Some of us have never understood any of those references to Macy's and Marks and Spencer's, but that never deterred *you*, did it? Never cost you a moment's sleep, neh?

That maiden-aunt chest! Those slumped shoulders! Teeth like tree stumps! Bum as big as all outdoors, you could save yourself from drowning after the *Titanic* went down by floating for a week in the icy storm-tossed brine if you had Mariette Planck's fat bum to cling to in the salty water!

As you can see, Sopwith judged the worth of his research assistant by narrow and bigoted criteria. Win a Miss Dairy Farmers contest in her one-piece Mariette might never, but she had a kind face.

Why did he keep her around the joint? Because while Sopwith was not brilliant, he wasn't stupid, either.

Mariette Planck was Sopwith's secret weapon.

Certainly he was embarrassed to be seen with her. Other television presenters spun through life in a sweet hazy cloud of long-legged sex kittens with master's degrees in library research, but they couldn't cut the mustard against Sopwith because Sopwith had a jewel without price.

While Mariette kept up her ceaseless stream of stunning, incisively researched program concepts, he was stuck with her.

"Thanks, babe," he said grudgingly. Sopwith needed her, true, but he didn't have to like it. He glanced at the notes on his desk and reached for his coat. "That share deal did it."

The gnome smiled up at him, pathetically pleased. "Sopwith, it wouldn't have counted for much if you hadn't brought it in so wonderfully right there at the end."

This was so, and he acknowledged it with a modest shrug. Unfortunately the attention seemed to inflame her. With a heave and a grunt she hoisted herself up onto the edge of his desk, a liberty he loathed, and lowered her muddy eyes.

"Still, perhaps you were a *little* bit naughty. He could sue the station, you know."

"Not a chance." Sopwith put his hand on the doorknob and left it there while he thought about what he'd said on camera. He'd followed Mariette's script, hadn't he? What the hell was she talking about? "Aw, Christ. Do you really think he's got an action?"

"Sopwith, I didn't mean to worry you! Sure, we'll have

to retract in a day or two, but you can work it in just before a sob-story and call it a clarification."

"Right." He groaned with relief. "Let the bugger stew in his juice for a couple of days."

Mariette nodded seriously. "He deserves it, the pig. Pity we can't use some of the *real* dirt I've got on him."

Sopwith looked alarmed again.

"Hey, babe, just keep me out of jail. The ratings aren't worth that much to me."

"You'll get there," she told him, putting out a hand and touching his sleeve. He jerked it away. "In a year there won't be anything you can't say."

It was like trumpets to his ears. Magnanimously, he overcame his revulsion and put his hand back, patting hers.

"Right. Right. Hammil the Crusader." He turned again for the door, eyes moist. "Well, see you tomorrow, kiddo."

Mariette pressed her small ratlike claws tightly together. "Uh, Sopwith? Do you have ten minutes to take your clever researcher down for a drink?"

He held the door half-open and tried not to break into a cold sweat at the thought. "God, I'm sorry, Mar. I'd love to, but I'm bushed. It's been a heavy week. Let's make it next Friday, with the guys."

"Lovely," she said, averting her eyes again. She found an unopened envelope on the corner of his desk and held it up. "Here, you nearly forgot—your tickets for the preview of Williamson's new play tonight."

"Christ, that's right." He'd already arranged to take Cynthia Belvue-Bennett to see Linda Ronstadt at the Starlight Club, and the bloody tickets had cost an arm and a leg. No freebies for Linda's show. That was drawing power! Williamson could wait.

"Look," Sopwith said expansively, "keep them, use them yourself, take a girl friend, whatever. I've got to get my head down tonight. Bye, babe."

He left her morosely tidying the office, and headed for

his lovely Porsche waiting in the underground car park in
his very own numbered and name-stencilled parking spot.

It certainly didn't occur to Sopwith Hammil that he was
destined for a meeting with a giant slice of kibble bread
from a forty-seventh century time machine.

Not that it would have done him much good if he'd
known. The future's one thing you don't have a *prayer* of
avoiding.

chapter four

The cell Hsia Shan-yun woke up in was dank, foul, almost lightless, and, she decided with horror, very possibly rat-infested.

This was impossible, of course.

The future's not like that. You know that and I know that.

The people who live in the future know it better than either of us.

Gosh, if a single fact has been established once and for all, surely it's that the future is *clean*.

It's sanitized.

Everyone's shoes are tucked neatly under the bed before they go to sleep, which they do at 10:15 or earlier.

The future's no banana republic. Granted, there's that little spot of bother immediately up ahead, with the ayatollahs and the pastors and so on, but nothing's perfect, not even utopia.

There simply can't be rat-infested cells with rusty chains and dried marks down the stone walls looking suspiciously like old blood (not all *that* old). The unions, the government, and the public service would not put up with it. The future is the last redoubt of *niceness*.

Hsia Shan-yun knew that as well as we do, which is why she sat there quivering with her hands jammed into her mouth and her white even teeth clamped into the skin of her knuckles.

She stopped after a rather commendably brief interval, and sat up straight on the wooden bench and stifled a cry.

She'd got a splinter in her bare arse.

Hsia Shan-yun shook her head to clear the fog out of it. A faint trace of illumination straggled through the tiny mud-caked barred window high in the opposite wall. It glistened from a rivulet of authentic dank running down the rough-hewn and palpably iron-hard blue blocks of stone of which the wall had been built, obviously by convict labor.

"Absurd," Hsia Shan-yun muttered.

Shivering, as you will when you are naked and you have lived all your life in centrally heated buildings and there's a nasty draft coming in somewhere, she dropped her toot-sies to the ground.

This was her next mistake, and she regretted it bitterly and at once.

The walls were not the only feature of the cell which were dank. The floors were danker.

Hastily, Shan-yun tucked her befouled soles back under her haunches and hugged herself tight to ward off the chill.

Hugging herself was something, it must be confessed, which she'd had a fair amount of practice in. Nobody else in her exceptionally silly world, 197 years ahead of Sop-with Hammil's, would give her a hug, so she'd had to develop a knack for doing it herself. Nobody hugs ugly people if they can possibly avoid it, and the people in the future were even better than we are at avoiding doing what might be nice for other people but grossly unrewarding for ourselves.

"Slimy floors," Hsia Shan-yun muttered in disbelief. "Barred windows."

What Hsia Shan-yun was experiencing has been de-scribed by the social psychologist Leon Festinger as *cognitive dissonance*. There was a big gap between what she believed and what she experienced.

After all, it's evident that Hsia Shan-yun found her ambient social order so entirely and unredemptively corrupt that she'd gone to the shocking length of planning to blow the crap out of its major data stores with a Striped Hole secreted within her own person.

Now, true, this desperate remedy was facilitated by her total lack of any sense of physical self-worth. If people often give you hugs when you're blue, or because they think you're nice, or just for the fun of it, you start to attend to the care and maintenance of your body. Blowing it to shreds to make a political point is the last thing that would occur to you.

(Is that true? Weren't the Baader-Meinhof Gang heavily into group gropes? Or am I thinking of the dusky people in berets who adopted Patty Hearst? Perhaps the reader can do the relevant research as a short paper and submit it later for partial credit. Send me a copy. I hate to get my facts wrong.)

Still, in her wildest vituperations against the State, in her maddest anarchic fantasies, Hsia Shan-yun had never imagined that they had become *this* barbaric.

"You evil malefactors," she suddenly screamed at the top of her voice, leaping from the bench into the slimy muck of the floor and beating uselessly against the unyielding stone walls, "let me out of here!"

This outburst was greeted by an equally sudden scream at her back.

All the tiny wild black hairs at Hsia Shan-yun's neck went rigid and tried to throw themselves overboard but got their feet caught.

She lurched around in the penumbral gloom. A second bench stretched out behind hers, depending from the wall opposite on thick rusted chains.

A dim figure, she now saw, huddled there also, naked and panic-stricken.

"Keep away from me, you fiends, or I'll tear your eyes out!" cried the voice, distorted by terror. Abruptly it broke, gave way to terrible wrenching sobs. "Do what you like to me, but leave my *mind* alone, you broggish snaggers."

Shan-yun was amazed and appalled. The dim figure was a breeding male in full heat!

She crossed the room in two athletic bounds, scarcely aware of the loathsome grime and squelching muck and pullulating pustules of decay and skin-crawlingly horrible fragments and so on stuck to the floor.

"Hey, calm down," she said urgently. "I'm a prisoner, too, honey-pong. Just woke up."

"Stay away," shrilled the breeder, arching his fingers into claws. He was quite a specimen, she saw. They must have been pumping testosterone into him for weeks.

"Flibble out, manjack," she said soothingly, trying to approach him in the skilled way a trained librarian deals with a maddened overdue borrower. She padded through the unspeakable vileness underfoot, sat on the creaking, swaying bench, started to put a comforting arm about the man's shoulders.

The claws flashed out and raked her face.

Fortunately, his nails were short and blunt. Even so, he nearly hooked out Shan's left eye with his pinky.

She slapped his flailing arm aside, caught both his slender wrists in one large hand, shook him heavily with the other.

"Listen, tooter, get a grip on yourself. I'm not a doctor and I'm not a State spy, and it looks to me as if we're both in the same flivver."

"A likely story," the brute snivelled.

Patiently, she said, "My name's Hsia Shan-yun and I'm here because I tried to do in a data store with a Striped Hole." That should give him pause. "What's your excuse?"

"You should know, you mendacious swine," he mumbled.

He was a nerdish little wimp, of course, due to the DNA-altering satellite radiations that had solved the world's problems fifty years before by making everyone kindly, socially responsible, aggressively peaceful, non-competitively self-regarding, and incapable of forgetting to give flowers on Mother's Day. Even so, Hsia Shan-yun now thought she detected a steely grace in his wimpish face, which was, for the reasons just adumbrated, fairly uncommon.

He looked at Shan-yun with watery eyes through which could be glimpsed some small spark of salvageable human worth. It was a wildly exciting sight for Hsia Shan-yun, given the narrow range of her experiences to this point in time.

"No, I don't know your name," she told him patiently, "and I don't see how we can be friends if you won't even tell me that much about yourself." There was no answer from the ruttish but miserable male. "Well, what *sign* are you?"

He still clearly supposed that she was lying.

"You and your henchmen must have been right through my brain by now! Why are you toying with me like this? Are you nothing but sadists? Get it over and done with, damn you. *Turn* me into a zombie. Rip out my brain and crush it in a *food* processor. Burn out my frontal lobes and peel all my other lobes down like *onions*. Ravage my—"

"Hey, ease up already."

"Shred my reticular activating system and unravel my cortical rind, do it! do it! and then just let me *go*—at least I'll be out of this horrible place."

And he was weeping again, wrenchingly, wrackingly, with the bitterness of newly found courage confronting archaic fears, of bravery facing down cowardice in the depths of the archetypal psyche, of ancient instincts battling with comparatively recently inculcated and historically untested utilitarian social values, of good against evil and sweet against sour.

Hsia Shan-yun spent several minutes wiping away the salty tears he'd got all over her quite large chest.

Even profound emotional breakthroughs into openness and trust must, sad to say, end.

Actually, Shan-yun's justifiably paranoid mind was starting to latch onto the idea that maybe this breeding male was the spy he accused her of being, that this primitive horror was some kind of carefully arranged and elaborate double-bluff to soften her up, damage her defenses, and cause her to spill out the names, addresses, and datacodes of her confederates (which she didn't have any of anyway).

She didn't get a chance to voice this unkind suspicion. Brain-fryingly bright lights glared on with a sizzle of ozone.

The wall—blue stone, dried blood, rusted chains, mud, slime, ichor, and all—slid gratingly up, one monumental piece, into the cobweb-matted ceiling.

A huge authentically ugly monitor robot hummed there on its knurled metal wheels, ruby dials flashing with menace.

At that very moment 197 years earlier, Sopwith Hammil was stepping out of his shower cubicle in his tenth floor Collins Street luxury bachelor unit, in the heart of the city. He grabbed a towel and applied it brutally to himself.

As Sopwith had been either indoors or inside his sleek airtight Porsche practically every minute of the day, you might wonder why he needed to wash himself at all. The secret behind this mystery is the apocrine gland system common to all adult humans of Sopwith's time period, and in fact for most of the time periods back to *Australopithecus boisei*.

Without doubt, sweat is the second-most disgusting substance emitted by human beings, and the only one of the two regularly displayed in public by people over two years of age.

This might strike you as a rash conviction on my part,

since perspiration is the method, as we surely both agree, by which primates regulate their temperature when they are not regulating it by the use of clothing, housing, air-conditioning, swimming, and open fires with merry marshmallows roasting on them.

True enough. But there's really no call to *stink*.

At puberty, human people right throughout history up to the time fifty years or so prior to Hsia Shan-yun's capture by the robot Bugs have sent little randy chemical messages to their most intimate parts.

The hormone messages say stuff like: "Grow. It's all right, do it. You might feel it's awfully embarrassing now, but you'll get used to it." And that's just what takes place.

Among the glands that put on their spurt of growth at this time are the apocrine sweat glands.

Don't confuse these with the eccrine sweat glands, which do most of the temperature regulatory work *and don't smell.*

That probably answers your first objection.

The apocrine sweat glands, on the other hand, like to advertise. How they work is this:

They live in human people's hairy parts, snug down near the follicles. Most of them congregate in unsavory places like groins and armpits.

That's the sort of glands they are.

Unreliable glands.

Uncouth glands.

Glands with a bad attitude.

I wouldn't want to go too far in glib condemnation of these glands. They are not work-shy, for example. The apocrine glands are only too eager to put their shoulders to the wheel.

The fruits of their industry are fatty acids that are squirted out through tubules the moment adult human people get out of control.

I could live with that. Fatty acids have rights. It's what happens then that turns my stomach.

Bacteria eat the fatty acids and leave bad smells behind. No kidding, they chew up those unsaturated fats and turn them into stinks.

A lot of smart people try to pretend that this is all right. They like sweat. So they say.

Sweat, for them, is an honest proletarian statement, a blunt showing of flags, a sturdy declaration.

They point out that in the *Encyclopaedia Britannica*, *perspiration* falls between the entry on *perspective* and the entry on *persuasion*.

Perspective is what we all want, of course. The states-man's long view, the insight of the informed. Winston Churchill had perspective, and he promised the British people "blood, tears, toil, and sweat." So the argument goes. I have to confess I do not find it persuasive.

Persuasion, of course, is exactly what sweat is all about.

A good strong whiff is meant to tell us that here is a human person with authenticity, with straight-up sexual earthiness. A human person who has laid it on the line.

This is what sweat persuades *me* of: that the human person in question is a pig who should go straight home and have a shower.

Anyway, it's not true that in the *Encyclopaedia Britannica* the word *perspiration* falls between the entry on *perspective* and the entry on *persuasion*.

The word *perspiration* is preceded by the word *Perspex*, which denotes a form of polymethyl methacrylate used for windows in old-fashioned Goggomobiles.

Perspex is a transparent barrier. A kind of synthetic protection from the brute force of Nature's elements.

I rest my case.

A cunningly contrived fan had drawn the billowing mists away from the faintly copper-tinted floor-to-ceiling mir-ror, leaving it flatteringly dewed. Sopwith was brisk with the towel, regarding himself sidelong with satisfaction.

His belly was flat, if not quite as flat as it had been in

his rowing days. Ninety minutes workout three times a week at The Man's Man saw to that.

He frowned. His Fiji tan was definitely fading. Better sign up for ten sessions under the Doctor Sunny or people would think he was working too hard.

Sopwith dropped the towel, kicked it into a corner where his cleaning help would find it, dabbed on deodorant and cologne.

The same people who relish the raw stench of sweat laugh like fools at the sight of other more considerate human people first washing off their natural sex signals and then splashing themselves with counterfeit sexual signals made out of ground-up dead animals.

These are people of defective sensibility.

These are people who take off their shoes when they get home after working all day in the hot sun and then sit in front of the television in socks that should be taken outside into the backyard and whipped.

These are people who laugh and jeer in the street as they tool past middle-aged joggers.

These people are, frankly, unworthy of our continued attention, and will be ignored hereafter.

Powerful waves of head-banging rock from Sopwith's compact disc player caused moiré patterns to dance in the dewy condensation on the big mirror.

He pulled his batik bathrobe on. The light in the bathroom switched off automatically fifteen seconds after he'd gone through the door. He had fifty minutes before he was due to pick Cynthia up. He crossed to the bar and started to fix a drink.

Something had gone wrong with the compact disc.

This is the trouble with technology. They give you a laser and tell you you can pick the disc up with your greasy fingers without affecting its musical clarity, but why should they be telling you the truth? What's in it for them?

It sounded awful, really awful.

Could this be Razored Eyeball's new image? With an eighties-style heavy-metal band, anything was possible, but it seemed unlikely.

What it sounded like, through the still-thunderous rock, was the high electronic bleating you get in the late late show's 1950 science fiction movie repeat to denote The Alien Horror.

These days they do that sort of thing with Moogs and Fairlight computers, and the BBC Radiophonic Workshop keeps five miles of tapes of it to stick into children's serials, so it doesn't have quite the same immediately creepy impact.

On the other hand, hearing something like that in the middle of your living room when you're alone ten floors up in the middle of the business section of a major metropolis and you're in your bathrobe and it's increasingly clear that it isn't coming from your expensive sound system, hearing something like a bad space-invasion film is actually rather alarming.

What Sopwith saw settling into his crushed-leather sofa, two meters long and shining of wax, drained the color from his heat-flushed cheeks.

What happened next sent a tremor of shock and incredulity through him. His grip on his glass slackened. Scotch and ice struck his bare leg in slow motion, tinkling and spinning like a banned cigarette commercial. The glass itself bounced several times off his shin, leaving a small but painful contusion.

Sopwith's uncomprehending eyes gathered in and forwarded without comment to his brain the following stimuli:

First, a hazy silhouette eddied into reality. It started out as gray smoke shot through with darting sparks of crimson flame.

The electronic piping grew shriller and hurt the roots of Sopwith's teeth.

"God," he squealed. He lurched back against the adzed cocktail bar. Glasses and bottles rattled.

An enormous loaf of crusty bread settled into real existence.

The top of the waxed paper enclosing it unzipped.

A single tasty slice of kibbled bread rose in much the way a piece of finished toast rises in an automatic pop-up toaster, except that it was too pale to be toast.

Sopwith knew instantly that this piece of bread, sliced insanely lengthwise, was an alien consciousness. Due to inadequacies in his upbringing, as we've noted previously, he erroneously identified its provenance as outer space, rather than the forty-seventh century, but he knew it was alive and he was pretty sure it was smart as a whip.

He waited, congealed, naturally, as you would be or even I would for that matter, with terror.

The slice of bread opened one blue eye and looked at him.

chapter five

I'm sure you've been wondering where O'Flaherty Gribble got to after his eager if somewhat embarrassing guest appearance on Sopwith's interview show.

This is the answer: the unconventional astrologer had a date with destiny a thousand kilometers away.

Within twelve hours, if his luck held, his hotly assailed hypothesis (the infamous so-called Callisto Effect) would meet its first definitive test.

This enthralling prospect was, then, in most respects the culmination of his life's work, for the Callisto Effect hypothesis threatened to overturn virtually every known doctrine of the Astrological Arts. Nobody would dare risk all on such a throw of the die without first being prepared and steeled to the task by three doctorates in independent disciplines, two diplomas (one of them for surf lifesaving), and a licentiate.

O'Flaherty had agreed to appear only on the understanding that Channel 8 keep a cab waiting outside the foyer for him. He dashed from the set the instant the commercial rolled, swiped the cosmetics from his face, and was whizzed up the freeway to Tullamarine Airport, where he caught the late flight to Sydney with a couple of minutes to spare.

By a strange quirk, the hourly Melbourne–Sydney flights of both major Australian airlines were scheduled to depart within five minutes of each other. This was the result of an interesting wedding between free enterprise and government control that acted to prevent either airline from suffering unfairly from competition at the hands of the other.

Human people living in Australia during this time frame were protected in a number of useful ways from doing things that might have caused them injury.

For example, they were not allowed to purchase "hard" mind-influencing drugs because to buy heroin or LSD made, distributed, and sold in accordance with the Pure Foods Act would have been dreadful for their moral fiber.

As a result, the rather small proportion of human people who wished to use these substances were encouraged by the government to break into other human people's private homes and remove all the portable objects they found there, especially videotape machines, and then take them down the road to shops where they could be exchanged for drugs. If the residents objected, the shit was to be beaten out of them until they ceased objecting.

Although this might seem a long-winded procedure, it had a number of immediate benefits.

It inspired a welcome spirit of enterprise in the community of drug users. This spirit had been badly sapped in other quarters by the unchecked spread of the welfare state.

It increased the market for new videotape machines, while ensuring that those people who could not afford new machines did not have to go without.

It meant that policemen could supplement their inadequate incomes by helping run this arm of the chamber of commerce without adding to bracket-creep or encouraging contumely toward the demands of the Taxation Department.

Best of all, it led to the swift deaths of many of the human people with an appetite for drugs, whose injected supplies could now be fortified without social censure with crippling bacteria, AIDS viruses, strychnine, ground glass, and other additives. This was desirable because most of the human people living in Australia at that time detested the drug fanciers for their hatefully heedless habit of bursting unannounced into non-drug-using people's homes and taking away, after first beating the non-drug-using people shitless, all the portable goods the original owners had worked long and hard to purchase.

O'Flaherty had decided on this occasion to travel by Australian Airlines, which was the less openly capitalist of the two airline companies. Australian Airlines operated on precisely the same business principles as its rival, Ansett, but was owned by the taxpayers of the nation.

It was a toss-up which of the two was the more boring, but I am here to tell you that the standards of cleanliness, service, charm of flight attendancy staff, and repair of the plastic internal surfaces of the aircraft were a damned sight superior to those found in your average American East Coast or United services.

Granted, the ticketing prices reflected these differences. It cost an arm and a leg to fly from any one point in Australia to any other.

On this evening, O'Flaherty sat himself down with a big happy grin in the first-class nonsmoking section of the Australian Airlines wide-bodied aircraft Flight 104 to Sydney, estimated time in the air a couple of minutes under the hour, and strapped himself in.

O'Flaherty Gribble loved flying. He had trained himself to have lucid flying dreams, which came to him at least twice a week, always in color.

He thought that perhaps in some previous incarnation he might have been a mighty hawk, swooping from its craggy eminence to tear some lesser creature from the naked winds and rend it, gulping down its salty blood in a primitive but ecologically responsible rapture.

Actually it is more plausible that O'Flaherty had been a Cabbage Moth in his previous life.

The Air Bus was half empty, thrumming with all the powerful surges of a late twentieth-century machine highly tuned to duty. Clean-cut sensible women in three separate designs of dreary institutional clothing wandered up and down the aisles, taking heavy objects from people and pushing them down on the floor in the space underneath the seat in front, or leaning across their faces to poke folded coats into overhead lockers or take light blankets or small cushions out of the lockers for the further comfort of restless or tensely sweating customers, or simply slamming the big curved plastic and aluminium doors of the lockers with a heavy, comforting clunking sound.

A man pushed his way past a flight attendant with short bleached hair and sat down heavily beside O'Flaherty, who was watching the small bright red and yellow and green lights outside his double-layered window with some difficulty, because the internal cabin lights turned his oval window into a slightly grubby scratched mirror.

"Evening, O'Flaherty," the man said, tugging at the groin of his trousers and trying to get his seat belt on without putting O'Flaherty's eye out.

"Why, hello," the astrologer said with surprise. He didn't recognize the voice, which was deep and growly and even more comforting than the confident comings and goings of the flight attendants. He hitched himself around and looked his neighbor in the eye, and still couldn't recognize him.

This was odd in itself, because as a result of his strange studies and even stranger life experiences, O'Flaherty possessed an eidetic memory.

In case you haven't read enough science fiction to know about memories of this kind, I should explain that people blessed with an eidetic memory are as likely to forget the face and voice of someone met for sixteen seconds seventeen years ago in a teeming Bangkok street as Dame Joan Sutherland is to miss the top note while she's belting out the Mad Scene from *Lucia di Lammermoor*. It's not entirely out of the question, but you'd be entitled to ask for a refund on your ticket.

"It's all right, O'Flaherty," the big fatherly man said with a grin, "we've never met. I'm familiar with your work, of course."

O'Flaherty felt his breast swell with pride and delight. He *loved* fans.

Most of the time he met knockers and mockers and crude ignorant people who wouldn't know their Aspect from a hole in the ground.

"I'm George Bone." His new friend looked like a combination of Orson Wells and Charlton Heston. "I saw you go through while I was buying my ticket, and took the liberty of asking the girl to give me the seat next to yours. I hope you don't mind?"

"By no means, George. Glad of the company."

In fact, O'Flaherty *was* a tiny bit put out, for all that he relished the chance of conversation with someone who knew his astrological work. Flight being O'Flaherty's dearest dream, he spent most of every minute he could manage in the air gazing lost and wondering out the window at the roaring open sky, the land so far below, the clouds hanging like great white whales, or shredded and wispy as his aircraft went into and through them, or huge and bulbous beside and below him as they climbed through the cloud layer for the quiet endless reaches of the sky above.

But you don't see much at night anyway, once you've left the runway.

"I caught the end of your appearance on Sopwith Hammil's show tonight," George Bone said, settling easily back into his seat. The NO SMOKING signs were lit and the flight attendants started to say stuff about small plastic masks that would drop into your face if the aircraft blew to pieces in the air. "Loved it. Vivid television, O'Flaherty."

"Why, thank you. Are you in media yourself?"

"You could say that, O'Flaherty. Hardware, software, firmware, wetware, all the media there are. But tell me, there was one thing you started to talk about and Sopwith cut you off—"

It had been the other way about, of course, and O'Flaherty's face tightened.

"If you don't mind, I'd rather not—"

"Ah yes, I have it," George Bone rumbled reflectively. The wheels of the plane rumbled with him, the engines shrieked, everything lurched, and they were away, and then the vibration was gone and the wheels clanged up and George Bone was saying, "Your research on the Callisto Effect, wasn't it? Fascinating work, will absolutely revolutionize the Art."

O'Flaherty could not believe his ears.

This man was an angel sent from heaven.

"You're the first person who hasn't laughed in my face," he said, mouth drawn down uncharacteristically.

"They laughed at Galileo," Bone told him.

"Yes, but they were Italians."

"The Callisto Effect," Bone mused.

"Callisto-Ganymede Effect, to be precise," O'Flaherty said. "The two major moons of Jupiter. Bigger than our own Moon, you know, both of them. Bigger than Mercury, in fact. Of course, Callisto has the greater impact on the horoscope, being in a larger orbit."

"You don't discern any influence from other moons, then? Apart from our own?"

"Well, I looked, naturally. There's Titan around Saturn and Triton orbiting Neptune, and Charon circling Pluto. But they're all too far away. Not a great enough angular distinction between them as they cross the horizon, though Titan only just misses the bus. Their planets mask the satellites' effects, you see."

"Coffee, tea, or milk? Or something from the bar?"
"Give me a Scotch. O'Flaherty?"
"Teetotal, George. White coffee, thanks."

Human people in Australia, even the aboriginal people who are often black as night, refer to coffee with milk as "white coffee." Visitors from Australia in countries such as the United States of America, where there are a large number of sensitive human people with dark complexions who until quite recently were chained together like dogs and treated worse, find to their chagrin that they are thought outrageously provocative when they order "white coffee" from a dark-skinned waiter. As a rule the waiter does turn out to be dark-skinned, as do the porters, servitors, and others holding jobs deemed unattractive for the dainty, which is very far from the case in a country like Australia where, due to a paucity of the dark-skinned, such jobs are done by working-class white people, these days often from countries in which one lot of more-or-less white citizens are blowing the shit out of another lot, or several other lots, of citizens similarly tinted, and being blown to pieces in return. In the United States of America, it is thought agreeable to ask for "coffee with cream." This means in practice "cheap powdered rubbish with pale thickener."

"You seem gratifyingly well informed on the Art, George," O'Flaherty said. He wiped coffee off his eyebrow. The plane rose and fell forty or fifty meters a couple more times and settled down to rock-steady level motion as if it had all been a bizarre trick of perspective.
"I have had an unusual life, O'Flaherty."
"Splendid," O'Flaherty told him with enthusiasm. "As you may know, I am a keen student of life in all its varieties. Perhaps we might pass the hour of travel most amusingly by sharing with one another some of the more

telling incidents that life in its richness has bestowed
upon us.''

"Another Scotch, thanks.''

"A refill, sir?''

"White coffee, thank you. And do you suppose I might
have some more of those delicious chocolate biscuits?''

"Which of us should begin?''

"Oh, you first, George, I should think. If you've read
my books, there's not much I can tell you that will come
as a surprise.'' This was disingenuous of O'Flaherty, as
we shall see. But the fact is, he really was tremendously
fascinated by the tales and trials and triumphs of others.
O'Flaherty was a great talker, once started, but he was
an equally fine listener. He settled back with a happy
smile of anticipation as George Bone threw down his second whiskey, leaned back, turned off the tiny spotlight
next to the NO SMOKING sign, which was poking him in
the eye with its long yellow finger, and began his tale.

THE STRANGE CIRCUMSTANCES
SURROUNDING THE TRANSFORMATION OF
GEORGE BONE

Had you met me at the time of which I speak [George
Bone began], you would have found me strikingly different in appearance. I was then a short stocky man with
hard hands and the squashy nose of a prizefighter. To be
candid, I probably looked like the sweaty oaf who steps
on your foot in the tram. Only those who knew me well
recognized the bibliophile whose collection of medieval
esoterica had spilled from my study to crowd two walls
of my living room, the sportsman who (quite illegally)
had bagged the ivory tusks decorating my fireplace. I
fancied myself a man who knew what he wanted. If I
could not have it immediately, I went out in search of it,
and brought it home.

On this particular evening in 19—, I had sworn to go
after the biggest game of all. And whereas in the past I

was staking my life, now I had compacted to stake my very soul.

If George Bone, stretched at his ease by O'Flaherty's side in the droning aircraft, observed the astrologer blench and start at these fateful and familiar words, he paid no attention, carrying on with his tale as though ghastly conjurations of the minions of Satan were the most natural topic in the world.

The acrid stench from the thurible [Bone continued placidly] made me wrinkle my nostrils in disgust. Hastily, I deposited a black tallow candle at each point of the large encircled pentacle I had chalked on my living room carpet, and went back to the kitchen for the salt and the saucer of blood.

I sprinkled salt at the cardinal points of the Double Circle and made a final trip to the kitchen to fetch in my musty, precious grimoire. I refreshed my memory on several points, closed the book, switched off the fluorescent light.

Saltpeter in the candles hissed and spluttered like tiny firecrackers. In their flickering light, my familiar room took on a decidedly eerie aspect. My pulse palpably accelerated, and I wondered momentarily whether I really ought to proceed with the conjuration.

Of course, I shook sense into myself, mildly angry at succumbing to what was, after all, surely no more than a barrage of primitive psychological tricks. A saucer of warm, fresh blood indeed. I reopened the grimoire.

Not for the first time in my life I was grateful that my tutors, unfashionably, had drummed the classics into me as a child.

O'Flaherty sent George Bone a brilliant smile of approval and fellowship.

"I too learned Latin and Greek in my childhood," he murmured. "Indispensable, don't you find?"

"Absolutely," Bone said, favoring the astrologer with a look that suggested he ought to reserve his comments for the culmination of the tale.

"Sorry," O'Flaherty said.

"Perfectly in order."

I placed the saucer inside the Triangle of Art, which would trap and hold the demon [George Bone said, once more taking up his tale], and drew an additional inner triangle in pure salt. Very carefully, I stepped inside my warded circles and closed their chalked perimeters. My magical apparatus was laid out as directed upon the cube of the kliphothic altar, all handmade and carefully engraved. They alone represented considerable expense in money, time, and dedicated effort.

Glancing at the page, at last, I let the Words of Conjuration of Demons and Lesser Spirits roll from my lips: "Acteus, Magelsius, Ormenus, Lycas, Nicon et Mimon," and a lot more in the same line.

Nothing happened, hardly to my surprise. Still, I felt my spine unkink a little. I felt I could abandon the whole rigmarole at that moment without compromise, but I was a methodical man even in my follies. Smiling a little, I brought the matter to its ordained close with the statutory Reversed Lord's Prayer.

"Amen. Malo a nos libera sed. Tentationem in inducas nos ne et. Nostris debitoribus dimittibus . . ."

A sharp detonation made me jump. From one flickering candle to the next leaped a violet spark, leaving in its wake a pale blue nimbus to veil each candle. Ozone reeked.

The saucer, I was pleased to note, remained untouched. Sweating very slightly, I continued:

"Terra in et, caelo in sicut, tua voluntus fiat; tuum regnum adveniat."

A modest black cloud of smoke was forming above the saucer of blood in the center of the Triangle, directly to the north of my circle. I stepped back, cautiously staying well within my encircled pentacle.

"Tuum nomen sanctificetur: caelis in es qui, noster pater."

The pyrotechnics had prepared me. As I concluded the satanic prayer, I took a good grip on my nerves.

A loud report shook the thick eddying smoke. I raised my eyebrows in silent speculation and dropped into a comfortable armchair, crossing my legs.

The smoke vanished. For the first time in my life I found myself looking upon a peeved demon. It was not a pretty sight.

The creature in the Triangle was seven feet tall and its naked scales shone like dull new copper in the candlelight. While the pointed ears and slanty eyes were traditional, the outraged expression was not.

The demon's right foot was ankle-deep in the saucer, and it was not amused.

"Why?" asked the demon rhetorically, eyes cast up to heaven. "Why?"

The creature gazed without relish about the room. In the tone of one forced to suffer fools gladly, it complained, "Isn't it enough to be dragged unclad from one's warm bed in the middle of the night, without having to stand up to my *knees* in *blood?*"

It did not suppress a shudder. "My *God,* what primitive creatures you are."

I confess that I sat at my ease, hands folded across my stomach, and heard out the whining demon with some amusement.

To assert that I had not been taken aback would not be the truth. This loquacious sprite was the antithesis of all the cunning hobgoblins I had encountered in my reading. But I was a man of broad capacity for intellectual accommodation, and I believe my aplomb was complete as I pulled out a packet of Camels, shook one to my lips, lit it. Filthy habit, I agree.

The demon's face brightened. "I thought they were banned."

"Not yet. Merely unfashionable. People are reluctant to die hideously of lung cancer."

"You don't object to lung cancer?"

"I have other plans." I inhaled luxuriously, controlling my spasm of coughing as best I could.

"Can you spare one?" The demon came to the edge of its Triangle and gave me a pleading look. "After all—the middle of the night . . ."

"Why not?" I saw no reason not be magnanimous. I tossed the packet across the chalked line, though I was not certain if it would pass the impalpable wall. The devil caught the packet adroitly. Its taloned hands shook with the excitement of an alcoholic who has stumbled on a half-full bottle. Pulling out two cigarettes together, the demon put them hungrily into its mouth and snorted them alight with a blast from its nostrils.

"Wow," it said gratefully, breathing out a thick wreath of greenish smoke from its incredible nose. It tried to lob the packet back; I was immeasurably relieved when the cigarettes struck the invisible boundary and dropped to the floor.

"I believe I have three wishes," I said.

"All right." The demon's poor mood was assuaged in the bliss of nicotine. "Let's hear them, and fair's fair. I am obliged to tell you that it won't do you any good." It leaned back comfortably on its tail, which had assumed a metallic rigidity.

Trembling inwardly with excitement, I came to my feet. I mentally traced the flowcharts of symbolic logic that had brought me, skeptic though I was, to this moment of sublime choice.

"*Why* won't it do me any good?"

Once more the demon was terse: "Look here, it's no

part of my duty to chew the fat with you all night long, you know. Make your three wishes and let's both get to sleep."

"If you wish to be formal about it," I retorted coolly, "my first wish is that you explain clearly and without prevarication why no one has ever been able to garner an advantage from an encounter of this kind."

For a moment the demon seemed about to collapse like a torn balloon.

"Oh well." The creature became philosophical. "I suppose it was inevitable. Semantics," it said. "The Whorf Hypothesis. The Ontological Pre-eminence of Symbol."

"Cut the cackle," I said sharply. "Be precise."

"The world is the way you look at it." The demon was reproachful. "Under certain conditions."

" 'Thinking makes it so'? But that just isn't true," I rejoined, becoming angry. "If it were, magic would be simple—and commonplace."

"It isn't true because of the Consensus Effect," the demon said. "Everyone else is also looking at the universe, which adopts the lowest common denominator as its Ground State."

" 'Everyone else,' " I mused. "Does that include you and your kind?"

The demon cast its eyes sidelong, shiftily. "Not exactly. We have our own universe."

You will appreciate the surge of excitement that galvanized me at that piece of news. "There's more than one?"

"Look, this is hardly groundbreaking material. I mean, what we're talking here is just a nonstandard version of the canonical Hugh Everett 'Many-Worlds' quantum interpretation, for God's sake. There's an infinite number of perpendicular universes, potentially. That's how the bloody 'Three Wishes' thing works, of course. We shunt energy from an empty universe through to this one."

"You still haven't answered my question. Why don't people's wishes ever succeed in gaining them what they desire?"

"Conservation laws. Don't you know *anything* about physics?"

In fact, my mind was working very fast. "Semantics," I said. "Consensus. Yes, I see that. So our two universes became coupled somehow—"

"An accident," the demon said bitterly. "A blind, dumb accident of symbols and words by some human buffoon in a dirty robe and a pointed hat. No wonder they called it 'the Dark Ages.'" It glared down at the saucer of clotting blood. "Not that I see any marked improvement."

"So conjuration opens a semantic path between our worlds. And I presume you're trapped here until the energy balance is compensated? Hence the three wishes."

"Not energy," the demon said testily. "*Perspective-equilibrium* would be a better term."

I stood up and stared hard into the demon's cat eyes, across the chalk boundary. "Is there any way around this conservation law? Anything you can do to make my wishes stick?"

The demon averted its eyes again. "In principle."

"You do want to go back home, don't you?" I must certainly have looked, for a moment, every inch the man who had blown a very large hole in the world's largest land animal and hacked out its tusks so that I might mount them on my living room wall. "I could keep you penned up here forever, I think."

The devil looked distraught. "It's no good, you'd have to use your second wish to get around the conservation problem, and then you'll only have one wish left. What if you regret your choice? They always do, you know. Invariably. Pitiful. Sausages on the end of the nose, genitals like mares—oh, the stories I could tell you . . ."

I don't mind telling *you*, O'Flaherty, that I knew with

a hot trembling joy that I was within an ell of the end of my search.

"Use my second wish in that fashion. A single productive wish is better than three futile ones."

The demon frowned. It raised its scaly hand, made a series of mysterious passes. The room shook. It bowed ironically. "Go ahead, then, dummy. There's a whole empty universe of energy waiting at your disposal. Make your third wish. Don't think I'll be around to help you out, because I'm heading straight home for bed."

With a stench of sulphur, the demon was gone.

I did nothing for a long time. At length I made myself a cup of strong coffee. Outside my windows, the sun was working at the lowest parts of the sky. My eyes itched. I considered going to sleep myself, the better to make my world-shattering choice with a clear head.

But I couldn't risk sleep. Freud. Unconscious wishes in dreams. Nightmares, for that matter. I blew out the candles. Curiously enough, their acrid stink no longer offended me.

This, you see, O'Flaherty, was the dream of my boyhood come true. The dream of my greedy, eager, power-lusting adolescence. The dream, indeed, of my dedicated maturity.

An entire universe of energy, the devil had said, and the devil had been constrained to speak only the truth.

It was undoubtedly possible, for reasons the demon had alluded to. Quantum physics, as far as my layman's knowledge went, bore the creature out. There might be an infinite number of vacant universes parallel to this one, void, waiting to be plundered.

Yet I could hardly fetch all that energy into my own universe. I might have a quasar on my hands!

Control. That was what I needed. Yet I could not waste an opportunity like this. Once was all. One shot.

What single boon could I ask for?

Perpetual youth? But I foresaw the dangers of being

caught out, imprisoned as a laboratory creature to be torn and probed forever by envious scientists craving a secret they could not copy.

Money? The economy could crash at any moment, and all would be lost.

Power? But what kind? Political? Sexual? I would always be sorry I had not asked for more.

"More," I muttered aloud. I drained the last of my coffee and put aside the cup. The answer was clear in my mind.

Everything. I wanted everything.

Unlimited energy, the demon had said. Very well, then, an unlimited wish.

"I wish," I said, slowly and carefully, "that from this moment forth every wish of mine shall be granted."

As the demon had vanished, so vanished then all the world, O'Flaherty, vanished noiselessly into the vacuum of its going.

Blackness was vast and complete.

I was pure ego, burning, alone.

The terror of loneliness assailed me, the misery of the utterly unknown. I stared across the unlimited territories of my own abruptly alien mind. I sought a stable starting point, and found that I was running, fleeing, lost and crying to a million echoes of myself.

My knowledge stretched on without limit, and without satisfactory focus.

Of course, I realized. Unconsciously, I had always wanted to know *everything*.

Fear shook me in my vastness. What of my other unconscious desires?

The darkness was infinity. I gazed into it and found only my own face.

Forever was a time that came and passed and was gone and lay ahead forever more.

Finally I could bear it no longer.

Aware of the consequences, fully conscious of it all, the

dreary pitiful pain of it, the moaning and shrieking and conniving and rottenness I was about to bring into existence, I knew what I must do.

I even knew on rather impressive authority what the words were that I must utter.

And there was. Light.

O'Flaherty looked at George Bone in loose-jawed amazement.

"You mean . . ." he stammered. "You mean you're *God?*"

Bone inclined his head.

"At your service."

chapter six

Chatting amiably at 15,000 meters over a cup of coffee with the creator of the local universe is one thing. Facing down a helium-cooled robot turnkey is quite another.

The Bug ignored Hsia Shan-yun. It fixed all seven of its nasty beady glowing red photoreceptors on the quivering person of the breeding male cowering behind her under his wooden bench.

"Ex-citizen Turdington Jimbo, it is my grave duty to inform you—"

"Aargh, aargh, *not the brainscrub machine!*" howled Hsia's companion.

"—that a final analysis has been made of your deviation," the monitor ground on in its unfeeling, non-Rogerian way. "In view of your intransigent recidivism—"

"My *what?*"

"You've done it before," Shan-yun said helpfully, "and they figure you'll do it again given half a chance."

"Oh. Gotcha."

"—you are to be taken to a place of correction where your unsavory personality will be expunged and replaced by one more to our taste."

"No! No! Not the scrub, you fiends!"

Ignoring every outburst, the Bug extended a small document featuring a really rather flattering three-dimensional picture of Turdington Jimbo with some of his friends at a take-out Japanese Nooky bar. No printing was visible, firstly because by 197 years from now nobody (other than intransigent recidivists like Hsai Shan-yun) could read, and secondly because robot Bugs see mainly at the ultraviolet end of the spectrum.

"You are to surrender this notification of intent to the officiating medic. Heavy penalties will attend unauthorized folding, bending, spindling, or mutilation of the card. Kindly follow me."

The machine spun majestically and rolled slowly away into the brightly lighted corridor.

Since one of its metal tentacles was firmly attached to the shrieking man's arm, Turdington Jimbo skidded across the foul, dank, slippery cell floor, kicking and banging with his spare arm.

The wall started back down again, with the intention of resealing Hsia Shan-yun inside the cell.

"*Hold* it, buster!" Outrage and disbelief made her own voice squeak. She hurled herself forward without waiting for that refreshing cortico-thalamic integration pause recommended by leading mental health authorities.

What you are about to witness is unadulterated thalamus at work. Brute beast.

Shan-yun rolled bruisingly into the corridor a split second before the wall blasted down into its groove with a crash that rocked the Bug on its tracks.

"Take your tentacles off him, you tin retard!"

The Bug spun about with dazzling speed, incidentally jerking Turdington Jimbo off his feet and slamming him against the corridor wall, which at least was smoother of surface than the cell's barbarous bluestone.

"Ex-citizen Hsia Shan-yun," it cried in a particularly official tone, training a scanner at her, "I discern that you are at liberty without lawful authorization. Have you taken leave of your senses? Return to your cell at once."

The bluestone wall at Shan-Yun's back screeched back up again into the roof.

Shan glanced over her shoulder. The cell looked even

less inviting than it had when she was pent up in it. She waited for the robot monitor to activate its spigots.

Watch closely, for we have come in this pivotal and revealing moment to one of the intrinsic limitations of artificial minds:

They are easily scandalized.

Some courses of action simply strike robot monitors as beyond the bounds of probability. I mean, would *you* leave your cell without proper authorization?

The Bug sat there humming, patiently waiting for Hsia Shan-yun to trot obediently back into durance vile.

The astonishingly tall, ugly, powerful woman again took advantage of this epistemologico-ethical programming flaw without conscious thought.

Robots have no thalamus, which might be why in the 1,482,965 worlds in the local arm of the Milky Way known to possess life, only one (Alpha Grommett) is governed exclusively by machine intelligences. Even that exceptional case can be explained, since it is now known that all mechanical life on Alpha Grommett evolved from an autonomic mousetrap discarded on the radiation-hot planet by a visiting Bargleplod seven million years ago.

Doubled over to reduce her profile, Shan-yun sprinted past the Bug and pelted up the stark white hallway.

With an efficient whine the monitor reversed, started after her.

Shan-yun dug her heels in, skidded to a stop, caromed off a wall, and headed back the way she'd come.

As her thalamus had hoped, the monitor had let Turdington Jimbo loose before it came after her. It could hardly hare off in pursuit with a living human person attached only by one arm, for though monitors had a disagreeable amount of discretion and no high regard for organic life systems per se, assault and battery was not part of their charter.

As a matter of fact, Hsia Shan-yun was betting her life on the truism, never to her knowledge publicly tested, that robots had an express prohibition against irreparably killing a human being built into their core chip.

She was almost upon it when it fired its cloud of gloop.

The stuff passed over her head, for at that very moment her thalamus had caused her to somersault forward, throwing her directly in the path of the monitor's heavy treads.

"Hsia!" the male screamed, hands pressed hard against his bloodless cheeks. "Oh, no! You'll be killed so badly they won't be able to *fix* you!"

Of course, the robot had jammed on its brakes the moment it worked out what was what, which as you can imagine happened pretty fast, given the niftiness of today's Large Scale Integrated Circuit chips and extrapolating forward 197 years from that.

Even so, it had acted too late.

The Bug was right on top of her. It did the only thing left to it. It lifted its entire torso into the air on its telescoping wheelbase, like something out of *Inspector Gadget.*

Hsia Shan-yun's thalamus was not working blind in precipitating this chain of events, because she had seen robots perform the same stunt to clear unexpected obstacles when moving at high speed. (I thought you'd like to be reassured that there was nothing gratuitous or ad hoc in her methods.)

She made herself snake-thin, or as close to it as a woman designed like Shan-yun could manage, by tightening her rib cage.

Treads clanked and banged and thundered past on either side.

She reached up convulsively and clamped her arms and legs to its underbelly, then clung on for dear life.

All manner of knobs and levers festooned the Bug's belly. Chortling merrily, Shan pressed, pulled and tampered with as many as she was able to reach with one hand, clinging the while to her haven. The monitor could hardly shoot gloop at her while she stayed in this position, but the depressing possibility remained that it might drop back down to normal profile and sandwich her across the floor.

A very bad noise went through her body then, like the bell of the Hunchback of Notre Dame being put through a suitably sized garden mulcher. This was followed by an equally abrupt ghastly silence.

The Bug stopped with a jolt.

Hsia Shan-yun fell off, banging her spine.

Somewhere farther up the corridor, the breeding male was venting strange muffled sobs. Shan rolled up her eyes, sighed, shook her head, eased out from under the motionless machine, and sat up to blow her nose.

Turdington Jimbo was not weeping with terror, as she had supposed. He sat in the middle of the corridor doubled up with mirth.

He was trying to hide his unseemly mirth behind his hand. When Shan-yun scowled bitterly, he only laughed the harder, shaking his own head in explanation and apology and gesturing for her to look behind her.

The monitor's twenty-seven utility tentacles stuck straight out from its torso like the quills on a porcupine. Its lights were off.

She'd killed it stone dead and turned it into a pincushion.

"Hsia," the man began.

"Call me Shan." To her amazement and almost without waiting to notify her brain, the stomach cramp of terror switched to a top-class pulse of sexual excitement.

"Turdington Jimbo," the breeding male said, covering his chest gallantly with his outspread hand.

"Hi. That's not—?"

"That's Jimbo."

"Gotcha."

Turdington Jimbo's eyes were shiny with the lust of the

reprieved. The erogenous zones of them both were inflamed, engorged, and highly visible. They were employing a form of signalling evolved by human people back in the days of *Australopithecus boisei* but hardly ever used to full advantage any longer because of the widespread custom of wearing clothes over most of them.

Instead of falling into an absentminded fit of procreation, though, Shan-yun ran to his side, grabbed his hand, pulled him to his feet. "Up, man. We've got to move fast."

"Don't be a spoilsport," Turdington Jimbo said sulkily. "Let's tango. Let's get it on. We could be big, really big. Let's talk this over. I know a great place where some actors go after the show, we could eat, maybe take a bottle of Chianti, or the house white's fine if you'd rather try something different, dance a little—"

Shan-yun slapped him hard about the chops. He staggered, touched his bleeding lip, shook his dazed head, averted his gaze.

"Sorry. You know how it is. I'd just like it to be the last thing I remember before they burn my brain out." He sat down again on the hard white synthetic flooring and started to cry.

At that moment the lights went out and the entire wall at the far end of the corridor lit up with the huge face of a gray-haired bureaucrat.

As enormous lips moved, an amplified voice like planks of wood being slammed over and over against the sides of your head told them:

"Do not make the slightest move! Nerve crunchers are trained on you both from every side. You will never escape!"

"Run, Jimbo!" Hsia Shan-yun cried. Hand in hand, lust and self-pity momentarily displaced from the center of their attention, they sprinted toward the huge projected face.

With a really awful teeth-grating whine, the nerve cruncher came on.

Hsia Shan-yun and Turdington Jimbo instantly crashed to the floor, while utmost agony knotted every muscle in their bodies into a macrame of incandescent thermite wire.

chapter seven

Roughly 197 years previously, burning twinges of neuralgia and deeply unpleasant surges of nausea were also afflicting Sopwith Hammil as he looked at the blue eye of the slice of alien bread which looked back at him without blinking.

The eye could not blink because it had no eyelid.

Blowflies have eyes like that, if you get very close to them and check out their heads with a magnifying glass.

The slice of bread that had appeared from nowhere regarded Sopwith with its single, huge, glinting, multifaceted, insect optical organ.

Cognitive dissonance inside Sopwith's poor simple-minded skull peaked at an overpowering off-the-scale reading, quivered for a painful instant, then twitched and collapsed back to a flat zero.

Sopwith had rejected what he saw.

This did not mean, regrettably, that the alien loaf of bread vanished clean away. The Principle of Reality by Consensus revealed to George Bone in 19— by a sardonic demon from a spare universe does not function that conveniently.

It is true that we are what we eat.

It is not true, thankfully, generally speaking, that we eat what we are.

Sopwith Hammil could not abide the tremendously morally threatening thought that he might one day, while absentmindedly reading the financial pages of his daily newspaper, butter and eat a slice of toasted alien with his breakfast coffee.

The Ontological Pre-eminence of Symbol swung briskly into play.

The hideous faceted insect eye stayed where it was, anchored definitely in time and space, glaring across his shag-pile carpet at him.

Everything else in its immediate vicinity swirled and shifted form.

Indirect lighting from the apartment's expensive fixtures were suddenly shooting green flashes back at Sopwith from his alien visitor's scaly chitinous skull.

Wicked mandibles clicked as the thing opened its repulsive jaws.

Sopwith simultaneously froze with horror and sagged with relief. An eight-foot-tall insect alien invader beaming down from orbit to materialize inside his living room was unbearable and certain to give him shocking nightmares for months afterwards, but it was infinitely preferable to a six-foot-long piece of intelligent alien kibble bread sliced lengthwise.

If you don't understand why this is so, much of our complex unfolding tale will slip deftly past your thick-fingered, irretrievably lowbrow consciousness. I suggest you take the book back for a refund and buy something by the Reverend Jerry Falwell instead.

Finally one of the messages Sopwith's trembling thalamus was sending to his lower limbs got through, even though it was flecked with the sweat of fear and expired shortly after. His limbs spasmed into action. He backed toward the door to the lobby which served four units in this tenth-floor penthouse-style bachelor complex.

You might wonder why Sopwith didn't seize the nearest firearm and blow the blowfly's head away.

One answer is that this was taking place in Melbourne, Australia, where the inalienable right to bear arms is not enshrined in a Constitution of Free Men under One God, and as a result of this deplorable oversight hardly anyone ever gets killed by the agency of a gun.

A second and more salient answer is that Sopwith's revolver was in the next room, in a drawer beside his bed.

Despite the widespread deficiency in the number of guns available to the Australian public so they might, as real men do, settle their differences without recourse to some goddam lily-livered and softheaded liberal court that was more than likely to award costs to any random malefactor after setting him free even though he's a faggot nigger, Sopwith did in fact possess a licenced firearm.

Australia was so backward a nation during this time frame that free white citizens actually had to seek police authorization to own and use a lethal weapon whenever they wished to. Just incredible.

Some months before, Sopwith had obtained his heat, his rod, his piece, his equalizer, after an anonymous but substantiated threat to his well-being.

Of course, the doors and windows of his expensive eyrie, including the key-operated door to the lift or elevator, were wired with the very best electronically controlled and radar-tripped protective devices on the market.

His sole mistake had been not to count on a shape-shifting alien intruder with the power to materialize on top of his crushed leather and hand-stitched sofa.

Sopwith's groping right hand suddenly encountered something on the bar behind him. It wasn't quite heavy enough or hard enough, but simply having something in his hand at this moment was enough to send a pulse of joyous relief through his frazzled shock-tautened flesh.

This desire to take up and hurl a fist-sized object was, by the way, a truly time-honored reflex stamped into the genotype of human people from events that had daily plagued *Australopithecus boisei*, a lowbrowed human person constantly affronted by sabre-toothed tigers, small warm-blooded dinosaurs left over from the Cretaceous, loan sharks, and the like.

Even as the glistening, mandible-drooling being took one short step for an alien toward Sopwith (but, as it turned out, one mighty leap for mankind), the lineal descendant of *Australopithecus boisei* clenched his hairless paw over the object, brought it up in a ferocious arc, and without further consultation with either his thalamus or his cortex, hurled it with every bit of the muscular force he'd developed in his biceps pumping iron three times a week at The Man's Man.

As it happened, the object Sopwith threw so murderously at his alien visitor was not well chosen as a weapon. It was the control planchette from his multi-room Bang & Olafsen sound system, a miracle of late twentieth-century engineering that allowed him to switch on, mute, amplify, change FM station of, activate either the orthodox turntable or the compact disc in, or turn off entirely his fabulously expensive Bang & Olafsen sound system with separate stereo speakers in each room including the lavatory. As a gem of Danish craftmanship and miniaturization, the control planchette was small enough to sit on a salesman's open hand and light enough to carry readily from room to room. In consequence, it's not what *I'd* have chosen to chuck at an alien intruder, but wealthy young media personalities no less than beggars can't be choosers.

There was a composure-shattering crash on the far side of the sofa.

Slashing through the alien's scaly skull as if it were not there, the control planchette, light as it was, ricocheted from the far wall, dislodged a signed Brett Whiteley limited edition print of a large brachiating primate, dropped like a plastic stone, and broke off the sensitive working end of the Bang & Olafsen tone arm.

The alien turned to inspect the damage.

"Really, earthling. Your behavior leaves a great deal to be desired," it said then, testily.

"Huh? Aargh? What?"

It glanced a second time at the ruined equipment. "Perhaps my colleagues in Doomsday Recruitment were mistaken in estimating your Stability Index so highly."

"You . . . you speak *Australian?*" Sopwith shoved his wet hands against the polished wood at his back, trying at the same time to still the humiliating trembling in his legs.

"Ja. Sehr angenehm, Herr Hammil. Vielen Dank für Ihre Gastfreudenschaft. Abfälle in den Mülleimer! Das stimmt so. Die Zweite links. Store ich?"

"What? Aargh? Huh?"?

"Oh. I thought you said 'Austrian.' "

"English," Sopwith shrieked feebly. "Australians speak English."

"My good fellow," the creature said with a minor but distinct note of contempt in its voice, "if *you* speak English, I shall do so. Our discussion would hardly be facilitated if I chose to address you in Basque or Mandarin." It gestured irritably at the bar. "Now look, get yourself a narcotic, or an ethyl beverage, or whatever it is you use to pull yourself together. We haven't got long before your sun goes out, and I have a number of other human people to attend before that doleful event occurs."

chapter eight

I trust it's abundantly plain that the sun was *not* going to go out and thereby plunge the whole world into icy Fimbulwinter, with the last pitiful remnants of starlit human life clinging hopelessly for a few fragile weeks or months to their grief-stricken life by the light and heat of those very nuclear power reactors that witless or communist-inspired ecology creeps (and their media dupes like Sopwith Hammil) had railed against as recently as scant hours earlier, before the sun was blown out as carelessly as a candle's guttering flame in the cold endless bleak infinities of intergalactic space.

After all, we know (even if Sopwith does not) that his insectoidal interlocutor is a visitor from the forty-seventh century, so the sun *can't* be about to go out, can it?

Actually, there's a flaw in that line of argument.

The slice of kibble that turned, under the blow of Sopwith's disbelief, into a B-grade sci fi monster *can scarcely be of human origin, can it?*

Picture this possibility:

Four and a half thousand years after our sad little brave little struggling civilization was puffed out by a gust of cosmic breath, a Galactic Patrol Police Special happens to be noodling through the starless wastes when it slams headfirst into a do-nothing, snow-shrouded black world going nowhere in the nothingness.

Annoyed and inconvenienced by the need to change their

wheel, the Space cops look the joint over for any possible infraction. It doesn't take their link with the staggeringly powerful but overweening Symbiotic Computer more than a few picos to lay bare the whole affecting tale, reschedule the cops to Archaeo-Forensic duty, dispatch their patrol hog back through a wormhole to the nearest available moment before the Big Snuff, and do a snatch on Hammil and a select sample of human people, a race never before recorded in the boundless annals of the boundlessly curious Symbiotic Computer.

Now, if that scenario has anything going for it, we could be in *big* trouble.

No, wait, aren't we forgetting something? Isn't Hsia Shan-yun a human person? And didn't she have the arm put on her in an era dated very nearly exactly 197 years *post*-Sopwith?

She is and did. You can relax.

But then, who ever stipulated that Shan-yun is living on *Earth?*

Isn't it feasible, and even *likely,* given what little we know of her circumstances, that she and the gray bureaucrat and Turdington Jimbo and the Bugs and all the rest *are the descendants of those few humans saved in the nick of time by the alien cops from the forty-seventh century?*

You see? Nothing is obvious in advance. In fact, that's intrinsic to the definition of science advanced by Sir Karl Popper, who maintains that the only propositions eligible for the sobriquet *scientific* are those which are in principle experimentally falsifiable. A strangely paranoid way to go through life, one might have supposed, but there you are. One corollary of Popper's widely endorsed definition, as you'll probably have heard, is that the course and fruits of scientific enterprise can't be identified ahead of time. Makes sense—if you haven't done the experiment that tries to falsify your hypothesis, you don't yet know if the universe is going to give it the big raspberry.

To cut all this high-level stuff short, I'll step outside the boundaries of discourse we've been employing up to now and tell you a little bit about the day *after* Sopwith Hammil's nerve-wracking interview with the alien from the forty-seventh century.

On the morning of that day, as the sun streamed like a benefice of gold into his Darlinghurst bedroom window, a biochemist named Joseph Wagner woke in a state of rare happiness.

Note the sun in this description. Fully on, no worries.

Joe yawned and stretched and sat up so he could survey the early morning Sydney bustle through the peaked gable window of his small bedroom at the top of a building used during nearly two hundred years for purposes either of prostitution or of procuring miscarriages through the use of an instrument, and now a boarding warren for students and unmarried post docs with a taste for sleazy living in the shadow of King's Cross, Sydney's famous hangout of strippers, bimbos, drug addicts, crime lords, karate hoons, artists, puzzled ageing working-class widows, and pharmacists with trained killer Dobermans.

The morning looked *wonderful*.

Joe bounded out of bed, grinned hugely, smacked his stomach resoundingly. It gurgled back at him but he didn't mind. This was the best day of the year. This was his birthday. This was Joseph Wagner's forty-second birthday, and what a beautiful morning for a forty-second birthday it was!

He leaped high into the air, clicked his heels in a genuine entrechat, and began a mad caper around his small paper-strewn bedroom.

That was a mistake, I'm sorry to say, because it gave him a chance to catch a glimpse of his face in the mirror.

His asinine grin pulled him up short.

"Forty-two," he moaned to himself. "My God, what a dream that must have been. Forty-bloody-two."

Joe climbed into a pair of old jeans, leaving on the slightly soiled underpants he'd worn in bed in lieu of pajamas.

"One more dreary day in a pretty dreary life," he apostrophized himself, striking a tragic attitude.

He went into the bathroom and splashed a flat handful of cool water into his face.

"Another existentially empty day tossing peptides from one test tube into another."

On second thoughts, he stuck his whole head under the tap and came up gasping.

"One more murderous day sacrificing rats on the altar of medicine in the attenuated hope of finding some wonder drug that all the bugs aren't already immune to. And what for?"

Like a drenched German short-haired pointer, he shook the water out of his hair, then dabbed blindly at his face and ears with a stale towel and groped wildly for a comb. It is instructive that at a time when all the other guys on the block were shaving their heads to the bone and dying the rest pink and purple, or plaiting their thick locks into spikes held rigid with Superglue, Joe Wagner still put a neat part each morning in his hair with a comb.

"Why," he answered himself lugubriously, "why, only to keep alive several million more crocks on a planet already long since hopelessly overpopulated. It's a wonder someone doesn't do something about it." He squinted sideways at the chortling sun dancing on the bathroom tiles and gleaming from the slightly corroded stainless steel fittings. "It's a shame someone doesn't just *turn the bloody sun off.*"

He looked at himself in the mirror and groaned. There was nothing much actually *wrong* with Joe Wagner, but all the different individual bits didn't add up to anything anyone would notice long enough to feel anything about. He was nondescript. He was *ordinary.*

Everyone wants descriptions, though. Here's one:

Joseph Wagner was a little under five five, dark receding hair (most of it lost since his last birthday, and damned unlikely to be there at all by the time the next one slopes past), close blue eyes weakened by reading and the fumes of industrial chemicals, the faint trace of surgical correction in his childhood of a harelip he believes to be a blindingly visible eyesore instantly repulsive to all women, and since it is women who excite Joe's sexual interest this is a real bummer of a belief.

He turned away, shoulders slumped.

Every morning this pathetic ritual is enacted: the confrontation with the mirror, the hunching of shoulders, the misery of an inescapable fate, the withdrawal of a tortured soul.

This is a life lived under the constant threat of impending blows. This is the stuff of tragedy and gloom.

But wait!

The sun still shines, its beams tease Joe Wagner's watery eyes, a bubble of elation dances its Brownian motion inside him, trying to burst free from the prison of his gray cortex and goose his thalamus.

Joe battled silently with his better instincts, tried desperately to plunge back into that slough of despond which was the accustomed safe shape of his life.

He crossed to the window, pulling on his drip-dry shirt and knotting its tie. A tawny cat stretched in the morning's first pool of warmth on the opposite terrace. It caught him looking at it and squeezed its eyes to the narrowest of autocratic slits. For the second time in a day, indeed in months, a big soppy silly happy grin spread across Joe Wagner's chops.

Still smiling, he switched the coffee perk on and then fried himself two chops and a couple of eggs for breakfast.

On his way downstairs to catch his bus, he passed his landlady. Shirl O'Toole was a shrivelled creature of indeterminate vintage. Joe smiled politely and she looked at him, he thought, rather oddly.

"Nice morning, Mrs. O'Toole."

"Yairs, isen it? Ow ya gown, dear, aw rite?"

As he passed through the front door he saw her still lingering halfway up the stairs, peering down at him with a curiously *hungry* look. Shrugging, Joe closed the door behind him and trudged up Palmer Street toward his Taylor Square bus stop.

The spring morning was alive with a sound-effects cartridge montage of inner city *mise-en-scène*. Even the grime of Palmer Street managed to poke and prod his eye with bits of life-affirming color. Trees and oxygen-starved but gamely blossoming shrubs in the little park next to the fish restaurant banged on his senses.

Joe loosened his tie, took a deep breath. Through the fumes, something good was happening. The effect surprised him. He pointed nose to sky and sniffed again.

On every side, the small things of life were putting on a gala show for his newly awakened cosmic, planetary, and municipal awareness. Two shiny brown-winged cockroaches made rhapsodic love in a crack in the pavement, shivering their tendrils at him, and Joe beamed back at them as he passed by without treading on them.

A junkie lay sprawled beside an overflowing rubbish bin, a needle hanging loosely from under his bloodshot eyelid, but even this familiar sight failed to dampen Joe Wagner's good humor. He flipped a bevel-edged coin to a news kid, took a *Herald*, dropped the thin back section of jobs in the wastebasket beside the rack of Mills & Boon romances and porno magazines, and stuffed the front portion under his arm.

This in itself was a major indication of mind-opening sensory driving, for Joe's normal pattern was to bury his head in the troubles of the world and try to forget he was alive.

This morning, without quite understanding what was afoot, he had eyes only for the warm brightening sky and the rusted lace of the terrace ironwork.

His bus was waiting at the light. Joe went straight up to the top deck. Instead of sinking into the backseat's obscurity, he bounced halfway up the aisle and opened a window.

From this vantage, if he'd been travelling along one of the more prosperous routes at the northern end of the city, he'd have had an unexcelled view right across the harbor, could have feasted his eyes on the huge arc of studded steel spanning a glistening expanse of blue, might have picked out a small churning ferry like a green-and-yellow beetle crawling on the face of the water.

As it was, a gust of grit went into his left eye and he had to prod it out with the corner of a handkerchief his auntie had given him for Christmas.

A blank-faced Vietnamese conductor took his fare. Joe slid the window shut and settled down to the crossword.

The bus filled quickly. Joe had decided churlishly years ago, after reading Germaine Greer's book, that Women's Liberation meant never having to surrender your seat to a lady. To carry this off successfully in the first years of the implementation of the policy it had been essential to develop a fixed attitude of psychopathic compulsion toward his newspaper, lest the sick, the old, or the uppity censure his lack of courtesy with a cruel look. Every so often he allowed himself a sideways squint through the window to check his bearings, and he did so now, fallen back into the torpor of habit through the torpor of habit.

The bus rattled down Oxford Street past the Victoria Military Barracks with its nuclear-targeted U.S. satellite controlling dish, through trendy Paddington still struggling awake after an evening of spellbinding dinners, imported cocaine, jaded sexual excess and clawing business deals, on past Centennial Park's beautiful huge expanse of lawn and trees and water and birds and joggers and Patrick White, the Nobel Prize laureate, strolling ruminatively, and toward Bondi Junction's shopping arcades and palaces.

During this traffic-jammed safari and panorama, Joe Wagner sought in vain for a twelve-letter word for "I think that furtive scratching means there's a mouse behind my bloody bookshelf," and felt the hair on the nape of his neck rising and rising until it bristled like one of those nylon brushes you use to get gunk out from under your fingernails after you've been fixing the bike.

His entire body was acrawl with the conviction that someone was looking at him.

Cautiously he raised his eyes.

He went red, then went deeper red, then went white.

His unconscious detectors, principally located deep in his thalamus, had not been kidding.

The young person directly in front of him, probably a girl with four quadrants of her hair removed and the stubble coming back in, had her neck craned well around to look at him.

The elderly lady with the big blue potted plant sitting next to him was looking at him.

Across the aisle, two middle-aged housewives on their way to Bondi Junction were craning their necks at him, one leaning heavily across the other to do so.

It was the work of a moment to establish that every other single pair of female eyes, which is to say two eyes each in every case, was also staring at him.

If his instantaneous response had been a spurt of embarrassment, it soon changed to a thrill of strange horror. Never in his forty-two years of nondescript life had Joe Wagner experienced anything approaching this concerted, calculated scrutiny.

He let his pental pen fall from his right hand, and his paper rustle from the nerveless fingers of his left. Delegating complete authority to his thalamus, Joe prodded desperately at his face, his hair, the outer surfaces of his clothing.

Had he, perhaps, left his trousers off? No, thank Christ.

Had some fiend sprayed his hair green? But that would hardly distinguish him from many persons half his age.

Eyes tightly shut, he considered himself and his situation in silent anguish.

Then he took another peep.

They were still peering at him.

He risked a quick glance over his shoulder.

Oh my God. More eyes. All female.

His scientific training reasserted itself smoothly, throwing him into quantitative mode. He started counting and categorizing.

Sixteen pairs of eyes regarded him maniacally, which is to say thirty-two eyes all up.

They were predominantly the eyes of young women: word processing operators risking RSI, he guessed, on the way to work; pharmacy assistants with degrees in aikido; several more married women with large raffia bags headed for the department stores; one old woman with long-established crow's-feet attending the organs in question.

The eyes stared, bovine, terrifying.

Joe Wagner ran through his personal inventory again. There was nothing wrong with his apparel. He felt at his features, palping the suddenly cool and bloodless skin. Ordinary. Forgettable. Lost in a crowd.

Had some notorious criminal with his face escaped during the night from Long Bay? Did he put people in mind of the Singing Rapist?

Joe Wagner felt a vast longing well up in him, a wish to pull the newspaper over his head and slink backwards down the steps and out of the bus at the very next stop.

"Here, what's going on?" a harsh male voice asked.

Belatedly, several of the men passengers had noticed the women's peculiar fixation. One or two, presumably married to, living with, relations of, or lusting after, the fascinated females at their sides, sent Joe filthy looks and muttered angrily to their companions.

The massed female gaze did not falter. The air shrilled

with some tension Joe could not name, never having been to a rock concert, let alone a performance of the late Elvis Presley in a Las Vegas casino.

A jungly scent travelled in a slow wave through the moving bus.

Joe gave up. A good-looking young woman sat three seats in front of him, a sun-bleached blonde with pale Bondi eyes. Joe made the best of it and stared back at her.

She began to hyperventilate.

Joe quailed. He had seen infatuated schoolgirls thirty years before when he'd been an infatuated schoolboy, even if they'd never been infatuated in his direction.

This lot loved him.

Every one of them. To the depths of their being.

They were besotted.

Joe covered his face with his hands, shuddering with disbelief.

He peeked through his fingers at the peaches-and-cream beauty up ahead and suddenly the tableau broke. With a squeal of uncontrolled joy, the young woman leaped from her seat, danced down the swaying aisle, and threw herself across his disgruntled neighbor and into Joseph Wagner's arms.

Instant uproar. Skirts swirled, leather pants creaked, baskets flew through the air as every woman from the pimply schoolchild in the front seat above the driver to the Italian grandmother swathed in black struggled to tear the lucky blonde off the astonished object of their maddened infatuation and keep him for herself.

The blonde was crooning suggestions which astonished him, hugging him, plastering his face with sticky possessive kisses. Behind her, beneath her, and over the top of her, a fight raged to get at bland, boring Joe Wagner.

The conductor arrived from the lower deck and added his hoarse and fairly incomprehensible question to the pandemonium. Husbands leapt into the fray and struggled to extract their maddened wives.

The laws of physics intervened.

The weight of people all struggling to force themselves into the one window seat on the top deck of a bus going around a curve caused the vehicle to lurch dramatically. Bodies crashed against glass and metal.

Groans and tearful crying added their emotional color to the uproar. Passengers from below began to force their way upstairs to see what was happening.

What was happening was that Joe was starting to choke to death.

The conductor, recalling tricks of the trade he'd used in getting out during the evacuation of Ho Chi Minh City, liberated himself from the mass of struggling bodies, grabbed a Melbourne visitor's furled umbrella like a sword and braced himself at the top of the stairwell. From this salient he was able to push the inquisitive from below whence they came and from time to time wield a pointed blow into the melee behind him.

Purple and losing consciousness, the object of the tumult tried hysterically to extricate himself from the pile of human bodies.

The blonde still clung to him and somebody else had grasped what remained of his hair, presumably with the intention of souveniring a precious nonrenewable resource.

Joe's cortex did not believe what was going on. It tucked itself away deep into the folds of his gray matter and counted sheep in a stuttering little voice.

In the nick of time, the ancient instincts of *Australopithecus boisei* forged to the surface. His chest swelled. He gasped air. The bus driver finally got wind of trouble and jammed on his brakes. Without a moment's thought Joe tore open the half window beside him, spasmed onto the seat, and went through the narrow opening like an irreplaceable cassette introduced by the postman through the slot in a letterbox far too small for it, except that unlike the cassette Joe was not hopelessly smashed into small ruined fragments. The blonde seized his ankle, but he jumped out and away like a slick frog at the moment the bus started to move off.

A broad canvas awning stretched from a Natural Health Vegan Goodery almost to the curb, and Joe's clawing fingers caught the edge.

He clung for an instant to the wooden strip high above the pavement. Astonished moonlike faces stared up at him, but not for long. With a tearing noise like the sound an insurance policy makes when you try to claim on it, the awning split down the middle and Joe tumbled head over heels toward the cynical concrete pavement below.

chapter nine

"Release the prisoner."

Hsia Shan-yun battled her way free of the lashing coils of boiling pain and sat up, looking blurrily at the gray face that loomed over her from the holovision screen. Its huge lips pursed in distaste.

"You cannot escape, Ms. Hsia. Mr. Turdington, to your feet, if you please."

Strangely unhurt, Turdington Jimbo climbed sheepishly to his feet and began to back away from his twitching companion.

"Sorry, babe. I know we could've swung, you dig? If we'd met in more propitious, like, you know . . . Love your glands, kiddo, no shit."

Shan-yun stared from the magnified image to the scuttling breeder and back again. She shook her head, which still felt as if it were connected to her neck by hot wire and staples.

"Ms. Hsia, I am your doctor. This psychodrama has confirmed beyond any doubt the analysis of obdurate deviation produced by the computers during your interrogation."

"What! You lying maniac, I haven't been interrogated! I only just woke up in that filthy cell—"

"The questioning was conducted while you were unconscious, naturally. This was praiseworthy efficiency, since the techbots had to anesthetize you in any case to recover the Striped Hole you had secreted about your person.''

Turdington Jimbo continued to skulk furtively down the corridor. Hsia stared at him with slowly dawning understanding.

"Jimbo! Is this prick telling me that you—"

"Just doing my job, honeyroll," he screeched. She was almost on him in one convulsive arm-swinging vengeful leap when part of the corridor wall bubbled, irised, put out a tentacle, and pulled him through, legs kicking in wild alarm.

The huge gray mouth in the screen pursed, sighed.

"You see? Utterly uncontrolled. You are a pitiful atavism, Ms. Hsia, a genetic error that we must set right."

Shan glared wildly up and down the corridor, prying at the walls and flooring with her strong fingers. The bubble was gone, sealed over. She was trapped, pinned down by the doctor's eyes, at their merciless mercy. Shan-yun's skin seemed rigid, her muscles shimmered, she seemed to feel every nerve picked out in blue and red and crackling with electricity. She looked like a wild beast with an IQ of 150.

"It is beyond the power of twenty-second-century mental hygiene conditioning to cure you. I have only one recourse left to me. You are to be taken from this place and—"

"Brainscrubbed!" The word burst like blood from her mouth.

"Certainly not! Do you take us for savages?"

Shan's lips did that rictus which cheap pulp writers describe as "a mirthless smile." It's certainly true that she didn't have much to chuckle about right at that moment.

" 'Brainscrub,' so-called, is merely a convenient fiction, serving as a public deterrent to deviation. We are not monsters, despite the detestable claims of your twisted philosophy."

"Your robot Bug said—"

"The KS-749 unit was programmed for the psychodrama that tested your fidelity to the State. Allow me to continue. You leave us no alternative but Hyperspatial Morphology Restructuring.''

You must have noticed the aggravating way bureaucrats and politicians love to simplify the genuinely difficult, handing out their jackass Golden Fleece Awards to people whose imagination and powers of thought leave them limping badly in the rear of the van of history, while inflating the commonplace with their orotund bombast.

In ordinary terms, what Hsia Shan-yun's doctor had in mind for her amounted to amputation of most of her limbs, surgical removal of all those items of her anatomy that distinguished her from her drab fellows, blurring of the eye's cornea to reduce her visual acuity, drugging and numbing of her mind, and in general changing her from the mind-crackingly ugly creature she was into a standard wimp of the late twenty-second century.

''When your physical state has been ortho-retro-fitted, you are to be taken to the Pacific Zone starport and from there removed to a place of permanent exile from the Earth, namely the Prison World ZRL-25591.

''In the company of other confirmed deviants you will live out what remains of your life in the perpetual absence of those advantages and regulations of civilization which you find so irksome. Judgment has been rendered.''

The man's face dwindled to a single point of light and then even that faded. The corridor lights went out, leaving Hsia Shan-yun in total darkness. There was a hiss of gas. It didn't make any difference to Shan. Even when you're in a state of hyper-arousal, ready to fight and die, red in tooth and claw, thalamus and cortex locked into synch, some prospects are simply too tacky to face while you're awake.

Having all your major bits trimmed off to fit you on the Procrustean bed is an example of one such challenge.

Even as the gas eddied into the corridor, Hsia Shan-yun was already out cold as a mackerel.

* * *

Approximately 197 years earlier, give or take a couple of hours or days, Sopwith Hammil was feeling almost as sick.

"The *sun?*" he bleated faintly. "Goes *out?*"

He turned numbly and poured himself a scotch over ice from sheer reflex. He stumbled with the tinkling glass to the leather armchair which sat side-on to the leather sofa, where the alien now swung one of its lower insectoidal legs negligently.

"Let me get this straight," the anchorman said, whiskey fumes gusting richly with every word. "You're from space, right? A creature from another world."

"Mind your tongue!" snarled the insect. "I do not appreciate the implications of your slur. Since we are obliged to employ your deficient and lamentably provincial language, I should prefer to be described—were it in fact the case, as it is not, that I haled from beyond Earth—as a *gentleperson* from another world."

Sopwith took very little of this on board.

He found the bottle still in his hand. This suggested pouring another slug. He was grateful for the suggestion, and used it. He downed the slug in a gulp.

"My gosh." He shook his head dazedly. "Out of thin air. The sun."

He forced himself to look the thing up and down.

It was worse than he'd first thought.

The oval, scaly insect head was the least alien aspect. The rest was just awful: segments of chitin, hairy multi-jointed stick limbs, a belly that seemed to hang down like the lapsed parts of an overworked swayback horse, except that it was covered with small pustular bristling chancres.

Sopwith whinnied slightly, poured, drank, belched, covered his mouth and then his face, shuddered rather a lot for a few moments, and then with the enviable recuperative powers of a trained television journalist who has seen more split and ruined pulpy human bodies in car accidents than most people have seen crushed cockroaches dragged himself hand over hand together.

"Sorry," Sopwith told the alien. "Please go on with your story. It was the shock, that's all."

"Why 'shock'? Parochial. Tasteless, insensitive, provincial, I say."

"I can't help it," Sopwith said with some asperity. "I've never seen a crea—a person from outer space before."

"I'm not from outer space, you imbecile," the monster shouted. "Do I look like something from outer space?"

Sopwith said nothing. Sometimes it's best.

"I represent a political faction in the forty-seventh century," the insect told him complacently. "Out of office right now, true, but we're making our comeback. Plenty of support out there in the hustings. Ordinary people aren't going to sit still much longer for—"

"Political . . . ." Sopwith muttered. His mind had seized on the first word he could relate to and rejected the rest. "Why me? Why not the Prime Minister? Industrialists, the guys with the real power? Anyway, why *Australia,* for God's sake? I'd expect you to be sitting in the White House or the Kremlin, what the hell are you—"

The insect snorted tersely. It gazed at the ceiling.

"If you were as astute as my colleagues must have supposed, for them to put you on my list, you'd grasp the reasoning instantly."

Sopwith's jaw sagged. For a moment one could be forgiven for thinking he was about to burst into tears.

"Well, I haven't the time to second-guess their judgments," the alien said huffily. "The line of thought is obvious. Think, man. The human creatures you itemized are well past their prime as breeders."

"That's not what I hear," Sopwith mumbled.

"I'm not interested in discussing their dirty little hotel-room secrets," the insect said haughtily. "We're talking species survival here, not hide-the-cabana. Your world is due to crash into long-term deep freeze in a matter of hours and you want to trade backroom scuttlebutt with me. Joseph Smith!''

Sopwith leaped to his feet. "The war of the worlds?" he shouted. "Invasion! You're planning to destroy the Earth!''

"Sit down you bloody fool." The insect drew from its breast pocket a thin cigar and shot him in the middle of the forehead with an intense thread of hard green light. A spike of frailty nailed Sopwith's brain. He collapsed voicelessly back into his wonderfully comfortable leather seat.

"Pay heed. I'll tell you this just once. Your sun's setting is about to be turned down by my political opponents in the Solar Energy Conservation Party. They'll leave the pilot light running, but your oceans will certainly ice up and most of the atmosphere will fall down within two weeks.''

"Why?" Sopwith cried feebly. "Why would anyone in the *future* do such a terrible thing to their ancestors?''

"It's not *that* hard to appreciate, I would have thought, even if they *are* my political enemies. What have you ever done for your descendants? Ripped them off, that's all. Used up their reserves. Pillaged the planet. Turned the nonrenewable resources into flat-screen word processors and Dolly Parton home video tapes. They're pulling the plug, Mr. Hammil, and though I can't condone them, I respect their right to their opinions.''

"I don't understand! Why the sun? Why not—I don't know, why not take all the uranium away or something? Aren't they against the misuse of nuclear energy?''

"Of course they are! What do you think the *sun* is, you cretin? A thermonuclear reactor. It's burning up nearly five million tonnes of gas a second. Do you have any appreciation of what sort of fuel bill that amounts to? We're talking 3.86 by 10^{33} ergs every second. That's not chicken feed. That's sheer *waste*, from the forty-seventh century viewpoint. Why should you low barely evolved human creatures get it all? Answer me that!''

The insectoid's spitted spray failed to reach Sopwith, of

course, being separated from his reality by a Hyperspatial Connectivity Warp.

"Hang on. These are *your* views, or the opinions of your political *opponents?*"

"My God, don't you *listen?* Do you think I like doing this? Would I be spending my Sunday evenings in a damned clammy hot environment like your filthy century for the *fun* of it? No. I would not."

"Just help me get this straight. Your *opponents* are the bad guys, right?"

"You know, Mr. Hammil, that is a . . . really . . . semantically *sophisticated* question. Dynamite. The 'bad guys.' You ask *me* if *I'm* one of the 'bad guys' or if my *enemies* are the 'bad guys,' and you sincerely expect a useful answer. Brother. Do they send me the dodos. Brother." The alien kept stopping in the middle of its diatribe to blow gusts of air from its mouth and shake its head from side to side.

Penitent, Sopwith mumbled, "Is there anything I can do to help you stop them?"

"Too late for that sort of thing now," the insect said briskly. "No. Sorry, we're well past the point where one could actually intervene in the *larger picture.* However—"

"Yes? Yes? 'However—'?"

"My time machine has ample space for a selection of human survivors from this era to carry on your species in a resettlement epoch. Hence, the answer to your earlier question. Tired party hacks are *out.* We're looking for young, robust, intelligent, forward-thinking humans."

Sopwith's gloom was dispelled. He felt his chest expand and his famous virile smile burst forth in his face. "And that's how *I* got on the short-list?"

"It's hard to credit, I grant you."

Sopwith's smile went away.

Oblivious, the monster added, "We've been watching your era's television transmissions and videotapes. The

Symbiotic Computer evidently found your image there and
notified my on-board drone that you were worth picking
up. I can't for the life of me see how it reached that conclusion, but then it has quite a lot more tadquarks in its
head than I have, and almost infinitely more than you, on
the evidence.''

"Perhaps there's an *environmental* connection," Sopwith offered hopefully. "Maybe you've been watching my
current special reports on uranium mining and damage to
the forests and the need for solar—"

"Enough chin-wagging. You will be fully briefed on
board. Now, fetch in your mate and we will squirt through
at once."

An awful clammy chill of foreboding and despair ran
through Sopwith Hammil's recently washed body.

"My—*mate?*"

"Holy Krishna! Your spouse. Your partner till death you
do part. Your better half. Your lawfully wedded. Your wife.
Your *mate,* you dense earthling!"

"I'm not married," Sopwith said in a tiny voice. "I'm
a bachelor."

The alien gazed at him as one might who has spied a
haddock's head discoursing on the meaning of Conserva-
tism in a Time of Troubles.

"Never mind," Sopwith added, rallying. "I'll be glad
to service the luscious brood mares you'll surely have
gathered together by now." He stood, reached for his
leather blouson. "What's keeping us, pal? Let's go."

"*Whaaat* did you say?" An insectoidal face can indeed
register moral indignation, aesthetic disgust, sociosexual
rage, and trans-species Sisterhood.

Sopwith recoiled. He cringed. "I'm sorry, I— That
is—"

"A travesty of ethical procedure! If I had my horsewhip
with me, young man, I'd lay it about your shoulders. You
dare stand there and boast of your readiness to copulate

with a female you are not mated with for life? For shame! For shame!''

''No, no, what I meant was—''

''Clearly, the Symbiotic Computer has made an error of the first magnitude. A colossal glitch. Never in 103 centuries and twice as many worlds have I heard such indecency!''

Brisk electronic piping sounded through the room.

''The recall signal. Time runs short.'' The creature's horrid outline shimmered. Its body faded casually from sight, and its voice thinned like the lonely, bitter sigh of a $600 million communications satellite falling uselessly from the Space Shuttle bay into the wrong orbit.

''I leave you the remaining scant hours of your life,'' Sopwith heard it saying, ever more faintly, ''to meditate on your abominable inadequacy as a family man.''

chapter ten

Sopwith was not, of course, the only conscious entity in the universe with problems of the heart.

Across the width and breadth of the whole Milky Way galaxy, through tens of thousands of parsecs and hundreds of millions of stars burning at rates governed by their position on the Hertzsprung-Russell diagram, except in the case of those stars that had been turned down by lunatic energy conservationists, beings large and small wept and wailed, beat their dorsal membranes against their cilia, wept salty methane tears, twisted and tore their soaked lace hankies, broke their hearts, plighted their troth, smurged and made up, loodled one another under cover of the Great Whistling Moon's descent, and in general got on with the business of providing material for the writers of Mills & Boon novelettes.

All happy families are alike, you see, but an unhappy family is unhappy after its own fashion.

Oddly enough, this was even true on Alpha Grommett, the sole known world in nearby space inhabited principally by machine intelligences.

Of a Christmas Eve, and indeed of every other eve, nothing animate stirred there, not even a mouse. Mice had actually been the first to go, on Alpha Grommett, which as I mentioned earlier was infested quite a long while back by the descendants of a single autonomic better mousetrap left on the innocent, fecund surface of the planet by a careless interstellar visitor.

Any self-reproducing machine, no matter how simple (and it's tricky finding one simpler than an alert mouse-trap) will mutate, given time.

Nothing mysterious here. No call to postulate a benefi-cent deity that has created living machines in Its own im-age. The principles of neo-Darwinism as upgraded by recent second thoughts on Punctuated Equilibrium are quite sufficient to account for the flowering of one paltry line of hungry mousetraps into the ornate, ticking, hum-ming, bright-cogged and copper-bushed mechanical ecol-ogy that today thrives on the denuded landscape of Alpha Grommett.

It is not strictly true that nothing organic lives there. Since 1937, a stocky green lizard with bifocals from the moist neighboring planet Gamma Globulin has held a quite important post with the principal newspaper in the capital city, Rock-Breaks-Scissors.

No reader knows her true name, of course. Fewer still realize that their favorite daily columnist is organic, and as you can imagine this is a secret guarded very closely by those few in the know.

By one of those droll turns of fate which play so regu-larly into the cynical hands of racists and bootboys, it has proved to be the case that nobody but an organic intelli-gence can pen a solid, moving Miss Lonely-Hearts col-umn.

Machines bleed, it's true. It may be lubricant rather than a thin watery suspension of platelets, erythrocytes, white cells, albumen, fibrinogen, floating nitrogenous wastes, and neurotransmitters on their way to and from work, but cut one with a welding torch and see if he doesn't bleed. Their pumps, no less than the human kind, can break with unrequited love; passion as well as Bool-ean logic seethes within their anodized chests; murders

and deeds of wild romantic heroism are done at lust's
behest.

Yet somehow they just can't rise to the empathy required by an advice columnist.

On Alpha Grommett, therefore, a retired upper-middle-
class brontomegasaur named Mrs. Emilia Aardwimble
reigns as the Heart-Balm queen for a whole world of tortured, lovesick, worried, faithful robot parents, children,
sweethearts, and suspected wirehead junkies.

On the morning I mean to tell you about, a morning the
dire events of which were to have such fateful consequences for all those involved, whose number did not, as
it happens, include Sopwith Hammil, Joe Wagner,
O'Flaherty Gribble, Hsia Shan-yun or any of the other
pivotal figures we have so far assembled, on this morning,
I say, a robot named Bruce Diode sat at breakfast with his
wife Sally.

They were not a happy couple.

"I may well be, as you allege, an old fool," observed
Mr. Diode. "You, by contrast, are a *frowdy* old fool."

He continued spooning graphite into his supplemen-
tary minerals orifice with one extensor, simultaneously
holding his novel open with a second elbow and slurping
light lubricating fluid from an oil can held in a third.
Between spoonfuls of graphite he expertly ground, polished, and inserted a fresh lens in his hind optic without
putting down his utensil or raising his forward optics from
the book.

"Well!" Repeated usage had long since worn the edge
from Mrs. Diode's indignation. "Sometimes I wonder why
I ever married—"

"—a half-witted buffoon like *you*," Bruce Diode intoned along with her, like a record. Their rituals were, as
robot conversational gambits tend of course to be, a trifle
mechanical.

Scooping up the last of the serviceable if hardly delicious thick gray dust, he slurped it down, keeping his

attention fixed on his book, nine-tenths lost in a glamorous if dangerous world of sharp crimes, tough PIs and incisive mouthpieces.

Sally Diode, on her side of the breakfast workbench, folded the morning paper from the funnies to her favorite column.

Early in their marriage, she had laid down her custom of reading the newspaper at breakfast. She had seen too many sitcoms of husbands blithely hidden behind newspapers to let Bruce get away with *that*.

While this gambit still didn't allow her to *see* her husband, she didn't particularly want to, not anymore. And the news was far more interesting than a running blow-by-blow account of the events in his latest sadistic cheap-edition thriller.

The truth was, their connubial conversation had quickly become reduced to a pattern. Each felt rather uneasy and more than a little miffed if the algorithm was abandoned. By running the same subroutines each day, they acknowledged each other's presence while avoiding the necessity of brute existential challenge.

Bruce rotated his upper optic the precise number of degrees inside the top of his cabinet to see the liquid crystal clock displayed there. Seventeen minutes to get into the city. He made an automatic computation. Eleven and a half minutes to reach the traction, drive to the office, park in the underground lot, ride the riser to the fourth floor, Bundy in, and lock on to his desk. That left precisely the apt interval to finish reading this next chapter and evacuate his discharge.

"You should be glad *anyone* married you," he said absently, varying the formula of their dialogue.

His hand touched the discharge tube, guided it to his ventral valve, clicked it in, waited for the negative pressure to build and activate the red light.

Flooding through the dome above them, the brilliant

X-ray-rich sun of Alpha Grommett kissed his cabinet without his noticing. His optics were riveted to the page.

Bruce Diode rather resembled one of the early treadle-driven Singer sewing machines, with random additions from tasteless Japanese war toys. He perambulated with some difficulty on four fat little worn wheels, preferring whenever feasible to transfer to the public traction hookup.

His wife Sally looked more like an Art Deco radio set, the kind that glow like burnished wood and smell like hot Bakelite as they warm up, their dial yellow and soothing as the purr of a tabbycat, station call-designations lettered beautifully on the illuminated half-circle of the dial and big chunky knobs to control sound and tone.

"Bruce! What you said—that's what Meg Kindheart says here to 'Fed Up,' " Sally exclaimed with surprise.

The tabloid, open at "For the Love-Lorn," dropped from in front of her dial with the snapping sound of abruptly folded paper. She studied her rusting husband intensely, amazed by his agreement with the advice columnist.

"Let's have no more about that damned interfering pest," Bruce said sharply. He glanced up with all optics from his thriller. Though his vexation derived principally from Sally's disregard of breakfast tradition, it remained valid that if he loathed one thing in all of Alpha Grommett more than any other thing, it was its sticky-beaking Lonely Hearts columnist.

"Pop psychology," he sneered. "Self-taught drivel. She should be deactivated for practicing witchcraft without a license."

"Really!" Sally was secretly glad of a break in the monotony of their normative programming, and anxious to defend her heroine. "Meg Kindheart is the most sensible machine in the world."

"Ha! You'd know about 'sense.' "

Mrs. Diode crackled a circuit breaker in a marked manner. "It's a pity there aren't *more* machines that show an interest in others." She cast Bruce a withering and significant glare.

He sneered back, racheting raspingly. "I wouldn't be surprised if the office cleaning Bug writes her rubbish." That stung, and he pressed his advantage. "And if it's not the Bug, it's some rusted-out old derrick that missed her chance fifty years ago."

He snapped his novel shut and clapped his hat on. "There's no one like a nonreplicating artifact to make free with advice."

Sally's dial went white. The numbers bleached. Her manipulators opened and closed convulsively.

"You—you old *bucket!*" she screamed and rushed from the room.

Bruce Diode sighed angrily as the door slammed, and spun his optic back to the clock. With a curse he found he was late. He scraped paint from his blower as he coupled to the traction. By the time he reached the office he was in a ripe mood. The hot humidity didn't help any. Bruce's routines had been disturbed for the first time in years, and his entire flow system was now out of whack.

Sally, for her part, winced at the crash of the traction's gears. Bruce was in a *particularly* unpleasant mood. Sighing, she returned to the lube bench and gathered the nozzles together. She consulted her own internal clock. He would be late for work. Sally flung the nozzles into the cleaning unit.

At the bench, she picked up the paper and finished Meg Kindheart.

Why did he have to go on like that? It hadn't been that way when they were first married. Self-pity dopplered through her and she wondered, not for the first time, whether they should have replicated while they were still new enough for mutations to be held within nominal limits.

The nozzles popped up shining and clean, and the emptiness of her life assailed her with crushing force.

Every day, the same recursive routine. She had become a drudge. Angrily, she damped her overload. What right did Bruce have to destroy her dreams? He didn't love her anymore, that was certain. All he ever thought about was his stupid trashy novels, his policemen and secret agents and steely PIs.

An awful possibility jumped up into her temporary cache memory. Could Bruce be having an *affair* with some letter-quality job in the office? Some fast, two-directional dot-matrix operator?

It didn't bear thinking about. A megabyte of ghastly, lurid bit-mapped images cascaded through her high core. Sally bent over the bench and gave herself up to her misery and shame.

Soon enough, her outburst ran its course. She re-booted herself, rolled to a mirror, regarded her artful if dated cabinet, the warm vacuum-tube glow at the back of her yellow dial.

"I'm not that old," she muttered. "Nowhere near the scrap heap, damn it." A fierce determination glowed in her deepest circuits. "I'll put a spoke in his wheel," she told her image. "He's not the only one able to play at that game. My days as his patient house drudge are finished for good!"

Sally turned and as her optics swung past the side panels of the mirror a cruel ray of the Alpha Grommett sun caught her worn knobs and tatty grille. Courage waned. She needed support; moral support for her new stand.

There was no question, of course, where she would seek it.

"Meg Kindheart! I shall write at once!"

Without further ado, Sally Diode found the modem keyboard and began pouring out her poor mechanical soul, all unknowing, to a lizard from steamy Gamma Globulin.

* * *

By midday, the office temperature was in the high hundreds. Bruce Diode, despite his insulation and autonomic regulation blowers, felt frazzled and short of temper.

Outside, he knew, in the mercury pools and mineral tailings, young machines cavorted under the roasting sun and thought of nothing but love, fun, and self-replication.

For Bruce, sockets running with oil, the day was the pit of hell.

All morning long, from its inauspicious beginning, he'd felt utterly miserable. He and Sally were well and truly stuck in a rut. He'd been denying this truth for years. Now it was unavoidable.

"Blast!" he muttered on the shortwave local band. "Damn and blast!" Several juniors raised their optics, shrank back to their terminals when he caught them at it. In a pet, he threw his files back into storage and seethed.

That bitch Meg Kindheart, he thought. What an inane name! She'd know what was amiss in his marriage, he thought bitterly. She'd give him a five-line solution, couched in such vacuous and elusive terms that it could mean anything or nothing.

Not that he'd ever read anything the fool had penned! Discharges, no. He leaned back wearily, letting his hind springs take the weight for a change.

Moiré static spun inside his CPU for a frightening moment. Inspiration struck like a glitch from heaven.

"William?"

The kid at the next work station shunted his optics cautiously. "Yes, Mr. Diode?"

"William, old knurl, can you lend me your copy of the *Intelligencer* for half a mo'?"

"Sure." The young mechanism looked relieved; he was not going to be shouted at. He fished inside his leg. "Here, sir."

Bruce nodded curtly, turned away so nobody could see over his shoulder, found *For the Love-Lorn*.

The office clock beamed out the midday break. Everyone but Bruce rose and left the room.

Mr. Diode drew a keyboard toward him and began a biting letter to the meddling machine he loathed so much.

chapter eleven

Some human people seize their problems boldly, as Bruce and Sally in their different if similar ways were doing.

Others just fold up.

Cower from Fate.

Look the other way.

Take a sickie.

Sopwith Hammil followed neither precept.

Seeing his last and only link to salvation thin out before his bloodshot eyes like disposable ectoplasm, he caught himself by the hair of his head, tore out a tuft, and bleated in fright.

"Stop that noise, man!" he heard the alien's faint, ever-more-distant, irascible voice tell him. "Show some dignity as you pass away with the rest of your kind."

"Wait! Oh my God. Oh my God. Wait! *You misunderstood!*"

He lurched across his living room, hands outthrust. the clutching gesture passed through the alien's insubstantial form in almost exactly the same way a beautifully acted, lavishly mounted Season of Shakespeare's Comedies passes through the television ratings.

"A joke!" he cried hoarsely. "A jest in poor taste! Of *course* I have a partner. *Every*one has a partner. Don't go. Don't leave me to freeze!"

The vague shape rethickened. Eight feet tall and scowling, the insectoid stared down at him severely.

"Frankly, Mr. Hammil, your humour escapes me. Still, when on Mars . . . Then you *do* have a mate?"

"Yes! That is, no, not formally—"

"What!"

"Wait! See, tonight was to be the night," Sopwith blathered, smearing sweat all over his forehead, "the night I popped the question. The girl I love, right? The young woman, that is. The *person*. To be married. Engaged. She'll say yes. I know she will. Been trying to get her bloody hooks into—"

"Hmm. 'Engaged'? That's not mated?"

"The next best thing. A mere judicial formality. And religious, of course," Sopwith babbled, "naturally religious also, any church or synagogue you care to nominate. Oh dear God," he sobbed.

The alien came to a decision.

"It's *something*, I suppose. But not enough. How much time do you require for these formalities?"

For five seconds Sopwith fainted.

A wave of relief, so profound it removed all the blood from his cortex and passed it, arm over arm, down into his internal bodily cavity, rendered him totally unconscious.

For another two seconds, each of them an entire universe of picos in which the Symbiotic Computer might have calculated the path of every galaxy in the universe from the Big Bang to time's indefinitely drawn-out conclusion, Sopwith's central nervous system endeavored to drag its tattered remnants into some semblance of a working party on the Problem of Human Survival, With Special Emphasis on the Survival of Sopwith Hammil.

Half a second later, by a triumph of homeostasis and good diet, his brain came back on line.

His spine straightened.

His bladder caught itself on the verge of involuntary emptying.

"Not enough time," he croaked.

"How long do you need? What kind of 'formality' is this, anyway?"

"Three days."

"Days? Right at this very minute the engineers are down there in the middle of the chromosphere fiddling with the thermostat and you think we've got *days* for you to fool around? Three hours."

Sopwith said something in a strangled shriek. He cleared his throat and said it again more clearly.

"Let's split the difference. A day. Give me twenty-four hours."

"Three *hours,*" the insect told him unbendingly. "Return mated and you join the survival-group boarding party. Otherwise I'll just have to leave one pair short. Roomier that way, in any case."

It started to fade again, amid sparks and smoke and electronic tones.

As it disappeared for good, Sopwith was certain that he heard, remote and malicious, its final, mean-minded stipulation:

"And make sure you bring the official mating document."

chapter twelve

If you ever find them coming at you with a Hyperspatial Morphology Restructurator, I can only advise you to run as fast as your legs can carry you in the opposite direction.

While you're running, search your pockets for a cyanide capsule.

If you find one, place it between your teeth and crunch down hard. With any luck, you should be dead inside a couple of minutes and beyond their reach.

Hsia Shan-yun was not that lucky.

She awoke stiff and sore. When she ran her hand over her aching face, nothing fit.

There are no makeup mirrors in a space-hulk, but once her eyes came as close to focussing as anyone can reasonably expect eyes to do when they've just had their corneas hyperspatially scratched out, she saw at once that the surgeons had really earned their fees while she was blotto.

Her legs were now slightly less than half their previous length, and effectively clubbed at the ends.

Shaking, she raised her hands in front of her weakened eyes.

Claws. Bird claws. Shrivelled, enfeebled things, the hands of a woman of 110.

Hsia Shan-yun moaned and tried to push herself to a standing position.

Every part of her body was out of whack. She tottered backwards, unbalanced.

When she looked down, a gust of shocked grief burst through her. Her breasts were *gone*. Under the rough convict sack, her chest was flat as a normal attractive twenty-second-century woman's.

Shan-yun started to cry. She slid woozily down to the metal deck and hunched there, puny arms folded over her poor depleted flesh. She sobbed with loss, then with growing anger, and finally with great noisy howls of furious defiance.

"Attention! Attention! We are now in orbit about Prison World ZRL-25591."

The throbbing in her head was not helped by the speaker blaring in her left ear. She covered the sides of her mutilated face with the mean little hands they'd left her, but the voice cut through like a surgeon's scalpel.

"Prepare for immediate disembarkation. When the doors open, leave your cells. Follow the green line to the shuttle pod. Attention . . ."

Howling with rage, Shan-yun shoved herself off the cold, damp metal plating and waited shivering for the snick of the door's lock. She was starvingly hungry. Her breath stank as it bounced back to her from the scratched, graffiti-covered door.

The door grated open. She burst out into the gangway and slammed into a surly woman with swarthy skin. Bristling, Shan raised her hands angrily.

And stopped.

Her entire physical relationship to the rest of the human world had turned on its head.

The other woman was centimeters taller than she, and tough with it.

Hsia Shan-yun dropped her hands and croaked, "You a fellow felon?"

The other woman lowered her own fists and frowned. "Freda Odell," she said. " 'Felon' is right. I was caught programming the teaching machines with subversive material.''

Shan-yun was impressed. ''Wormhole theory?''

''Nah. History.''

They smiled and hugged each other with spontaneous warmth.

''Move along! No loitering!''

A green arrowhead flashed imperiously along the scarred metal bulkhead. Shrugging, the women followed it to the shuttle pod.

Seven other sociopaths were already there, looking lost. Nobody was speaking to anyone else until Shan and Freda arrived, and they'd hardly begun to liven the party with introductions and outbursts of grievance when another PA system started up.

''Enter the shuttle in orderly procession! Strap in at once for immediate re-entry. Hurry it up. A nerve-crunching for the tardy!''

''In a pig's eye!'' Her moment of rational humility firmly behind her, Shan-yun started along a side corridor looking for someone to kill with her feeble new hands. Worried, Freda lingered at the entrance. The rest filed in obediently.

''Back to the shuttle, deviant!'' yelped the PA. ''At once!''

A single jolt from the nerve cruncher convinced Shan that she was in neither position nor shape to seek immediate restitution. Somewhat cowed, she limped back to the shuttle and allowed Freda to strap her in to an acceleration couch.

The trip down to the surface was done under power, a monstrous buffeting racket that lasted ten minutes or ten hours and more or less precluded conversation, plotting, thinking about sheep or indeed any activity more demanding than being dead.

Hitting dirt in a shuttle is like having a golf club slam your spine, though this simile would not have occurred to Hsia Shan-yun. Golf was outlawed under the All Islamic–Christian Decency Interregnum as morale sapping, and never regained its popularity owing to the brief but concentrated use of major greens for disciplinary rallies.

Shan did wonder, though, how many uses the authorities got from a shuttle before the bloody thing fell into small pieces from sheer mechanical fatigue.

Nauseous, the six women and one man in the convict landing detail, assuming I have the penological-cum-military terminology correct, stumbled from their landing couches and lurched down a creaking plastic ramp for their first look at the place of exile.

The planet was *hideous*.

"Hubbard's E-meter!" Freda was appalled. Her fists tightened at her sides, and Shan-yun could hear the knuckles cracking. "It's . . . it's—"

Hardened subversive that she was, covertly trained in the lore of the history of human people on and off planetary bodies, Freda could not bring herself to express such an indecency.

Shan gritted her teeth and forced out the words Freda Odell was looking for.

"Open. It's *open!*"

She could hardly breathe. The blue, white-splotched, hazy ceiling infinitely high above them was, she decided through her viscera-clutching panic, what the people of Earth used to call "sky."

Just thinking the word was enough to throw her into a tizzy.

The insane visual distances on every side put her already blurry eyes completely out of kilter. She simply could not conceive of so much open, unroofed, unused space.

Browns and greens and yellows and other blotches of visual stimuli lay here and there with no sense to them.

Hsia Shan-yun was experiencing the exact opposite of the Ontological Pre-eminence of Symbol. Here and now, brute empirical reality was crashing over her sensory input systems, bypassing the usual interpretive codes and grids.

She saw stuff she couldn't name.

In fact, she saw stuff she couldn't, strictly speaking, even *see*.

"Give it time," she murmured desperately, trying to hold Freda vertical as the larger woman toppled toward her in a faint. "Our ancestors dealt with this. We're just as tough. Freda, there are some people coming toward us. Freda, I think we're going to have to be on our toes, kiddo."

The human people walking in their direction across the uneven dirty floor had come, Shan finally appreciated by dint of a bout of sheer intellectual effort, from the squarish slope-topped boxes a few hundred paces distant.

"Buildings," those things were. Dwellings constructed "outside" from dried organic tissues. "Wood," that was it—"wood."

Most of the advancing party of human people were males, and each of them looked approximately the way Hsia Shan-yun had looked before the surgeons had got to her. True, they were not two-meter-tall Valkyries, but their limbs were visibly swollen with muscle. Compared with the shuttle wimps, they could have been a different species.

A tremendous screaming thunderous racket burst through the air.

Shan spun on her heel, which hurt rather a lot, and what she saw took the last bit of gristle from her backbone.

The shuttle—the sole decent, human, metal, *manufactured* object visible on the entire planet—was blasting off from the surface.

Freda shrieked. The man in their group keeled over and lay facedown in the dirt.

The flame-cupped shuttle soared like an ancient god, diminished from mere human ken until it was a bright dot immensely high in the blue.

Freda too quietly slumped to the ground and curled up like a fetus.

"Hey, come on, snap yourselves together!"

The strangers, by one of those incomprehensible tricks of perspective, were abruptly in their midst, pushing roughly through the group, pulling and slapping and punching the newcomers to their senses.

Shan-yun stared.

Cracked faces, seamed from exposure to the open environment. Eyes like archival holograms of animal eyes, startlingly bright in the raw sunlight.

One of the men shook her shoulder. In disgust, she threw off his hand. He wore garments made from dried animal skins and woven vegetable fibers. Shan felt tiny creatures, real or imaginary, scuttle out of the clothes and crawl all over her own bruised skin.

"Right, you motley crew." The oldest of them, a man whose face was half covered by an appalling wild growth of pubic hair and whose sunburnt scalp was covered by an equally appalling huge patch of baldness, stationed himself in front of them, fists braced on hips.

The male convict, awakened and tottering, took his first close-range look at the kind of creature he was now doomed to become, and spontaneously vomited into the dirt.

"Clean the bastard up and get him to the med shed," the leader snarled to a subordinate. "Now listen up, you people. I know what you're going through, so I won't be too hard on you straight off. We've all been through it. You'll live—unless, that is, you die, which isn't impossible."

* * *

Are you beginning to zoom in on the picture? There's always a standard lecture along these lines which everyone in a frontier-planet type situation has to listen to at some point. Man, the toughest, meanest critter in the entire goddam galaxy. Who seeds the universe must preserve elementary savagery. The blood of patriots watering the tree of liberty. Stirring stuff, not to be missed. I'll put a short bibliography at the end of the book for anyone who's new to this game and needs to catch up. For the rest of you—relax, chums. I'm doing what I can to tool right along through this little number. Back with Joe Wagner in a moment, I promise you.

"We haven't got the spare personnel or the resources to coddle you. Everything you eat, your housing, your antibiotics, your drugs, your entertainment—you'll make them yourselves."

"I don't know anything about any drugs," one of the convicts cried pitifully.

" 'Housing'? What's 'housing'?" asked another, with a sob.

"You'll specialize, naturally," the old man said. "What you don't know now you'll learn—or you'll die." He seemed to relish this prospect, smacking his lips. "There's no place in this outfit for crybabies and lily-livered liberals. You'll have to be tough—tough, and determined to *survive.*"

He stared from one convict to the next, squinting in the bright light. Hsia Shan-yun felt as much like vomiting as I do. But she met his gaze when his eyes reached hers.

He locked on to her, tried to stare her down. Shan's pupils shrank and her whites boiled with blood. He grinned with satisfaction and pointed at her.

"You. Round them all up and bring them across to the Great Hall when they're ready. We have to get back to the harvesting. The Big Wet's due any day now."

With a gesture to his companions he turned and started back toward the wooden buildings.

"Just a moment," Shan-yun said loudly. To her ears, her voice seemed attenuated, an auditory shadow of its former power. Was it the atmosphere of this world, she wondered, or yet another atrocity wrought by her doctors?

The man paused elaborately, glanced over his muscular shoulder, narrowed his sun-dazzled eyes.

"I take it you're addressing me."

"I want to know your name," Shan yelled.

"My name's Anson. You can call me 'Boss.' We'll talk later." He turned away again.

"Hold it, damn you." Shan-yun tried to stride like a tiger toward him and managed a dwarfish totter. Even so, he stiffened, and his men moved in on either side of him. "What's the escape plan?"

Anson grinned sardonically, then slapped her painfully on the arm.

"I like your style, sweetheart, even if you do lack a little something in the looks department. I think you're going to do all right here on Paradise—if you learn some manners."

"The escape plan, Anson."

"No escape, lady. The shuttle comes here once a year. Remote control from orbit, Bug driver, nerve crunchers from New Year's to Christmas. There's *no* escape. What was that name again?"

"Hsia Shan-yun, snotsucker."

He grinned, and she recoiled at the sight of his thin hard yellow gums, his missing teeth. No cosmetic dentistry on Paradise.

"Unless you just happen to know how to plait a Striped Hole, my dear foulmouthed ex-citizen Hsia, you're *here* until you *die*. Until you rot and we put you in the ground."

Shan-yun ran her tongue around the inside of her mouth. By an odd oversight the surgeons had left her all her own teeth. She bared them happily at Anson, and strolled away to round up her companions from the shuttle.

chapter thirteen

Joe Wagner fell from the sky like a stone.

Fortunately, he fell like a stone that was wrapped up in the tattered corner of a heavy canvas awning. Slowed, rolling, flailing his arms, he knocked down a fat bystander and felt the air *humph* out of his own lungs.

Relieved and terrified, he pushed himself off the fat man's supine body. The sight of Joe's face, white with fear and covered in smeary lipstick, robbed his victim of words, which was certainly a stroke of luck.

Some other fool was yelling shrilly for the police. The sounds of running feet came distantly into Joe's shock-stopped ears. Shaking his head in disbelief, he stood up groaning, then bent down again and helped the fat man up as well.

As fat men will, the fat man stood openmouthed and speechless, gathering volumes of blood into his lardy face for an apoplexy.

Shreds of canvas whipped about Joseph Wagner's ears. A hysterical store owner berated him, waving a sturdy stick of celery menacingly over his reeling head.

Women began to gather.

Lots of women.

Lots of lovesick, increasingly frantic women.

Joe cast about, spied a taxi twenty meters away at a light. Fearful of a riot in the street and worried about the police, he made an unashamed dash for sanctuary.

The cabdriver gazed at him laconically.

"You the bloke jumped outa that bus," he reported.

"Yeah." Joe surveyed his soiled clothes in dismay. Something struck the side of the cab. A young woman in a mac, probably a holidaying visitor from Melbourne, tried to get inside with him. He jerked in fright, pushed down the door lock next to him, leaned across and did the same to the back door on his side.

The light changed.

"Look, get me to Purity Soaps, will you? There's a tip in it if you put your foot down."

"For a feller jumps outa bus, I do it for *nuthin'*, mate." The driver slammed his foot on the pedal.

Despite his early exposure to the foolish and distastefully sexist fantasies foisted on young male human people during this time frame, Joe found nothing gratifying in his ridiculous adventure. On the contrary, there had been something utterly disquieting, even horrible, about his experience in the bus. Wiping the lipstick from his face, a physical reaction hit him. Huddled and shivering, he could make no more satisfying response to the driver's ear-pricked straining silence than a flattened, tight-gutted silence of his own.

There wasn't a woman in sight when the taxi pulled up to the curb before an old brick building with less than the customary number of windows and rather more of pipes, outlet vents, and smokestacks. Taking no chances, Joe peered cautiously around before he unlocked and got out.

He stared for a moment at Purity's reassuring dirty brick wall, then thrust a bank note into the cabby's hand and bolted inside the plant.

Relief washed through him. He was entering a world of science, where the laws of physics and chemistry were rigid, measurable, conservative, and certainly not about to permit any further outbreaks of ridiculous amorous miracles.

Just to make sure this was so, Joe slid through the door on the first floor and ducked past his secretary before she had a chance to go glassy-eyed.

He leaned against the inside of his closed door and panted.

After a while he opened his own glassy eyes and checked to see what was what.

His office, and the several small rooms of the laboratory beyond it, were as ever. No horde clamored up from the benches or burst from the animal cages where his small friends and victims resided, chittering at his arrival with either pleasure or terrible dread, depending on which theory of animal rights you hold with.

The habits of years took command, soothing him, but not before he prized his back away from the door and turned the lock.

He pulled on his white, stained lab coat, switched on the fans, and slumped into his chair.

What had it been?

A mad dream?

The trouble with calling it a dream was that you were stuck with the adjective.

Joe swallowed. A hard lump remained in his throat.

He shook his head. Lunacy should be retained as the explanation of last resort. If anyone were insane, it was that bunch of broads on the bus.

Hey, wait a minute! *Pheromones,* maybe?

The idea burst up like a jolly blop of gas from a geyser's bubbling ooze, and made him smile in delight and relief at his own stupidity in not seeing it sooner.

"Pheromones," he muttered. He rushed to his tatty piles of *Nature,* biochemical journals, annals, all the bumph of a working scientist, and began rooting with no trace of system through index pages.

"Glands," he croaked. "Sex attractants. Scent trails. Moths. My goodness. Chemoreception. Territory markers. That's it. Of course. I've done it by accident. Fleming and Florey. A Nobel Prize, by golly. Altered my own metabolism somehow. Something I spilled last week. Damn it,'' he cried happily, flinging paper into the air, "I'll be famous! I'll be able to ask for a raise!''

I don't think it can be denied that Joe Wagner was jumping the gun in his outright enthusiasm for this hypothesis, but who can blame him? As an elegant solution it certainly seemed to fit. I mean, look at mouse piss. *Smelling* mouse piss would actually be more to the point, at least if you're a mouse, but let's look at it anyway.

Male mice piss not only makes lady mice bay at the moon, it brings on their estrous cycle like nobody's business. Sound familiar?

Excitedly, Joe hauled out his log and pored over his work notes for the previous days and weeks, searching for a clue to the chemical miracle that must have turned his entire metabolism into an incendiary beacon for the opposite sex.

It couldn't be his piss, he decided.

Yes, he slept in his underpants. True, he wasn't the cleanest young person ever to come out of a Sisters of Charity primary school. Still, the effect he'd induced in the women on the bus was *fresh*. It hadn't been turned on the day before, and he'd been wearing the same underpants then.

There was nothing relevant in his notes.

There was nothing that said he'd made some rapture, some essence, some filthy-minded erotic fragrance that turned him into the male human equivalent of a female gypsy moth.

Carried on the wafting air, tiny eeny-weeny bits of female gypsy moth pheromone fetch in the blokes for thousands of meters, and *they* have to battle upwind.

Joe sniggered to himself. Rich! Rich!

A single female silkworm moth spurns Chanel Number 5, swearing instead by a sex attractant called "bomby-kol.'' Brother. Let me tell you. You won't believe this.

How much bombykol does the single cruising silkworm moth carry in her purse? Point zero zero one five of a gram, is the amount.

Not a bucketful, I think you'll agree, but then, she doesn't need much.

Her point zero zero one five of a gram is sufficient to haul in a thousand million freaked-out sex-crazed males, assuming there happen to be a thousand million male silkworm moths in the neighborhood, which hardly ever happens.

A smudge of ugly mold once turned out to be penicillin, and went on to save millions of lives and probably cause the population explosion.

Joe quailed at the thought of what the Wagner Male Pheromonic Factor would do to the population explosion, but he stopped quailing after the briefest statutory moment. Fame! Fame!

Carefully, he copied down the empirical formulae of all the substances novel and conventional that had been across his bench top in the past six months.

He put his work notes back in the drawer, washed his hands carefully, and drew on a pair of surgical gloves in the complicated method used for surgery and barrier nursing.

He took smears from his skin.

He breathed into glassware and sealed away his breath.

He scraped gunk from his tongue, fore and aft.

With a shamefaced glance at his locked door, he dropped his pants and rubbed slides across his private parts, also fore and aft. He sealed these samples carefully and pulled up his pants again.

He drew blood from his thumb.

He ripped out some hairs.

Then he went to work with his expensive equipment.

The scanning electron microscope turned his smeared

exudations into grainy maps of the Moon, but this time the Moon was inhabited by squirmy little critters made of shadows on a television screen.

He stared and compared. He brought the magnification up and lowered it again. Nothing. Nothing worth a Nobel, at any rate.

He did things to the breath of his lungs with Nuclear Magnetic Resonance and though the protons flipped their spin on command they told him no news of value.

The phone rang several times, but Joe Wagner didn't hear it.

He failed to hear the knocking on his door, either, and after a while it went away.

He prepared cultures on Petri dishes and set them aside to divide, grow, respond to test antibodies and fiendish chemicals.

Nothing.

His metabolism was functioning normally in every respect, as far as scientific instruments could detect. He didn't even have a cold.

Finally he sat on a four-legged stool and stared at his hands. He'd almost lost sight of the insane problem that had got him going.

Maenads. Maybe it was just that he looked like some rock band three-day wonder, the lead singer with the Slashed Eyeball or whatever they were called.

Would a little old Italian granny in black rush like a urine-stoned mouse at the lead singer of a spike-headed band? Not really.

Maybe it was a virus.

The guys in the cages behind him were yelling for munchies and a cuddle.

Sighing, Joe went across and extracted Fat Mac, a handsome devil with a reddish gold tail. The animal jumped eagerly in his hands, expecting a tidbit. Smiling, Joe found a lump of sugar, which the monkey ate with small clean bites, holding it in his tiny black human hands.

Anything important enough to infect Joe Wagner and turn him into the on-board sex symbol for an eight o'clock Oxford Street bus had a fair chance of infecting this small, bright creature.

Fat Mac didn't like the needle. Joe gave him another piece of sugar.

This is also the way human people reconcile other human people when they have just done something really abominable to them.

A second way is to do another really abominable thing to them very quickly, often with a piece of padded pipe.

A third way is to allow them to hold elections from year to year. This used to be thought extremely subtle, but going on the evidence it isn't as effective as the second method.

Maybe it's just not as much fun to administer.

Joe put Fat Mac back behind wire, isolating him this time from the two females and one other male that made up his primate pool.

Lunch hour came and went. The females in the next cage groomed each other stoically. Fat Mac mooned about his cell, scratched, picked at his food. Joe ran his hands desperately through what was left of his hair. He was hungry and he couldn't go out.

The lady monkeys yawned and painted their nails.

Between Joe and his lunch stood his secretary and a probable gauntlet of women crazy for his body. If it was true. Unless the effect had worn off. Unless he was a suitable case for treatment.

"I'm as clear as a bell," Joe said loudly, to hear how it sounded. It sounded pretty plausible, if you allowed for the fact that he was talking to himself. "Four and a half hours of hard lab work, all of it impeccable. Nothing mad there, ha ha."

This was not convincing. Joseph Wagner knew as well as you do that insanity is not that simple.

You don't necessarily go about dribbling and frothing and gibbering.

What about Sweeney Todd? Shaved all day and hacked all night.

A sample of scientifically attested pheromone-free sweat burst forth from Joe's forehead.

This time he answered the phone.

His secretary's voice, responding to his presence through two layers of thick wood and a sheet of corrosion-proof metal, was coy and honey-sweet.

"A man out here to see you, Joe."

I could say she cooed, and I would not be lying, but would you forgive me?

"He says he's a . . ." Her voice faded for a moment. "—'thaumaturgist,' whatever that is."

Joe gazed at the passive female monkeys. Fat Mac, he noticed, was attending to his own problems. "Tut tut, Fat Mac," he called. "For shame."

"Beg pardon?"

"I'm very busy, Enid."

"He says he has to see you straightaway."

"What's his name? Not the chap from the Bondi Junction Natural Health Vegan Goodery is it?"

He heard more muttering. He had no idea what a thaumaturgist was, but it didn't sound scientific. That is, it *did* sound scientific, but since he'd never even *heard* of the discipline it was probably some damned crackpot marginal area. Chiropractic, say, or worm poo ecoculture like that fool had been promoting on Sopwith Hammil's show the night before.

"He just says it's very urgent, Joe."

"Oh, all right, send him in."

"I can't. Your office door is locked." Usually she would have snapped this accusation at him. Today she sounded like some pouting queen of kinky sex from a video nasty.

"Sorry, I'll be right there."

Enid was thin and proper and in her late fifties, but she was standing on tiptoes holding her chest out, hoping to be invited in to Joe's love nest. A man stood in her shadow.

"Come on in. No, not you, Enid. Please, Enid, think of your position. Quick, damn it, slip past while you—"

Joe slammed the door and clicked the lock. Breathing hard, his flushed, ecstatic visitor stood staring at him through bottle lenses that fairly glowed with admiration and self-satisfaction.

"I was right! You're the one!" the man cried in absolute delight. "And in my lifetime! The Callisto Effect! Allow me to wish you a very happy forty-second birthday, Mr. Wagner, and many more to come."

"Hang on, I know you," Joseph Wagner said. "I saw you last night on the box. The bullshit artist!"

"The same," cried O'Flaherty Gribble, "but surely you mean *wormshit* artist," and he took the astonished bio-chemist by the hand and pumped it like a proud father of newborn twins. "I'm so happy to meet you at last."

"You are?" Joe cried. "Me?"

Could this jackass have found out so quickly about the women? Yet what other reason could there be for the country's most controversial astrologer to be here, shaking his hand with the zeal of a municipal counsellor standing for re-election after just selling off all the public parkland to the local soccer club?

"You, Mr. Wagner. You."

"And what's so special about *me?*" Joe said in what he hoped was a skeptical bark, though he was horribly afraid, in his heart of hearts, that the fellow was about to throw open the lab door and release a hundred maddened women at his throat.

"Special? My dear Mr. Wagner," O'Flaherty Gribble declared, infectious as a bug and twice as lively, "or may I call you Joseph?"

"Joe."

"Joe, I believe I can put it quite simply and directly. As of today, as of your forty-second birthday, why, you just happen to be the single most important person in the world!"

chapter fourteen

On his way by air to winkle out Joseph Wagner was where O'Flaherty Gribble had been, of course, the previous evening, when he'd had his illuminating conversation with George Bone.

"Something similar happened to me, actually," he told Bone.

"Really?" George Bone said, smiling back at him with paternal unconditional regard.

"Well, I suppose you'd know." But O'Flaherty's mind, sharp and clear as honed glass, couldn't but help him make the crackling mental jump to a tiny incongruity in what he'd just heard. "Um, if you don't think it impertinent of me—?"

"Ask away," George Bone said genially. He reached up and pushed the button that brought the flight attendant down the aisle. "Another Scotch, thanks, and something for my friend here."

"What will it be, sir?"

"Do you have mineral water?"

"Ice-cold Perrier, sir?"

"Fine." She trod away in her sensible shoes. "That's what I was about to ask you, sir," O'Flaherty said.

"Yes, I see that. You're wondering why I offered you a drink when I should have known you're teetotal."

O'Flaherty smiled shyly and nodded.

George Bone sighed, patting O'Flaherty's hand. "It

doesn't work that way, you see. I'm only human, after all.''

O'Flaherty looked sidelong to find out if he were being joshed.

"Really, son. I may be boss cocky of this local universe, but I can't be everywhere at once, can I?''

"I always thought that, well, you know, that was part of the job description.''

"Medieval metaphysics and wishful thinking, I'm afraid. Thank you, my dear.''

He drained his Scotch, and the color heightened in his cheeks. He really was a tremendously impressive fellow. You'd trust him with your life savings.

"It's done via ASCII-standard menus and indexes, O'Flaherty, so I can find my way around without having to flick the cards one by one through eternity. Admittedly I've picked up a fair amount about people. I'm a pretty deft judge of character, which saves a bit of effort. But for the fine-grained detail I have to go through the literature search and the filing index just like everybody else. Well, of course, nobody else has *access*, but that's one of the perks, isn't it?''

O'Flaherty was looking downcast.

"Oh. I was hoping you might be able to clear up a few matters that've been bothering me.''

He turned away and looked into the deep night sky. At least in first-class you're well forward of the wings, so the flashing lights don't interfere with the view of the sky. Far below he saw a faint dusting of lights. Some minor rural town. It was not really easy to grasp that this was all the handiwork of the man in the neighboring seat, but there it was and it was so. He knew that much beyond any doubt.

"Fire away, son. Spit it out. Always willing to listen.''

"Um. It's just that— Well, some of the things that happened to you seemed awfully familiar, that's all.''

George Bone looked at him sharply.

"Diabolism? Three wishes? I can't believe a nice young man like you would dice with the devil, O'Flaherty!"

The astrologer smiled again and shrugged his shoulders.

"George, I really thought you'd know all about it. In fact, I thought that's why you were here talking to me."

"Not to my knowledge, O'Flaherty. Pure coincidence, as far as I can tell." George Bone grew thoughtful. "You're right, though. It *is* stretching things rather. I wonder what . . ." His voice trailed off. He looked O'Flaherty in the eye. "Would you mind terribly if I read your mind?"

"What, actually got inside and—"

"Access the files, Peripheral Interchange, won't hurt you, I promise."

"Why not?" cried artless O'Flaherty Gribble with a grin. "I've got nothing to hide from you, have I?"

"Unless I have your freely given, informed permission, O'Flaherty, your soul's a sealed book to me. Only ethical approach."

"My gosh. Yes. I'm most impressed. I never really thought of the creator of the universe having high ethical standards."

"We all falter, O'Flaherty, but I do what I can to keep up to the mark."

George Bone sighed again, and it seemed for an instant that the very fabric of the aircraft shook like cheesecloth. The pilot's PA hummed on briefly, he cleared his throat, thought better of whatever he'd been about to say, and got back to flying the plane.

O'Flaherty felt a rush of sympathy for Bone. He reached over and patted his knee.

"It's all part of our agreement, isn't it?" he said. "You told me your story and I was going to tell you mine. This just saves my throat a lot of wear and tear, eh?"

"Bless you, O'Flaherty. You'll hardly feel this." George Bone picked up O'Flaherty's right hand and held the fingers lightly. "STAT B:*.*," he said.

For an instant, a small hurricane blasted through

O'Flaherty's inner brain, traversing both thalamus and cortex in the merest jot of a second. He seemed to behold an endless sweeping list of memories, events, faces, places, ideas, choices, actions, and failures to act, each categorized neatly by file name. It took far less run-time than even the superlative Symbiotic Computer of the forty-seventh century would have required. Bone was correct. It didn't hurt. On the other hand, it definitely felt quite queer.

"That was it?" O'Flaherty said breathlessly.

"No, no, I was just running a status check through your index. Had to make sure what was there. Okay, this won't take long. PIP."

A deep clear pure beautiful tone immediately said: "*"

"GOD:=GRIBBLE:*.*," said George Bone, and it was so.

Everything O'Flaherty Gribble had ever *been* drained in a gigantic gulp of several thousand gigabytes of thought and emotion straight from his soul into George Bone's capacious repositories.

As Bone had promised, however, this copying process left O'Flaherty exactly as he had been at the outset, in no item or byte diminished, though with a slight ringing in his left pinky.

"Ah, I *see*," George Bone said, leaning back to digest O'Flaherty's life. "I *thought* your name was familiar."

THE MAGICAL HISTORY OF
DR. O'FLAHERTY GRIBBLE

Gribble Senior [George Bone now understood in a total flash of divine recall] had been president of the Moorabin Stake of the Church of Jesus Christ of Latter-Day Saints in Australia when young O'Flaherty was old enough to be a deacon.

As an Aaronic teacher, the boy marched from door to suburban door with an elder of the Melchizadek priesthood, brandishing his copy of the *Book of Mormon,* only to be hounded into the street, often enough, by rough Irish Catholics, or invited in to tell his tale of salvation, without ultimate issue, by some pathetic pensioner visited by nobody else from one year's end to the next.

After endowment he never went anywhere without his temple clothes, the ritual underwear that protected him from sin. He learned to spurn coffee, tea, alcohol, and fornication. He found nothing strange in the fact that beneath his parents' suburban Melbourne house was a large carefully prepared cavity stocked with enough food and supplies to see the family through a full year of tribulations when the Last Days arrived.

None of this, on the other hand, did him any spiritual good whatever.

When Gribble Senior had graduated in Utah, years earlier, in business administration, he was already a "seventy" and, by the time he got back to settle down in Melbourne, looked a likely choice for bishop of his Moorabin ward.

Young O'Flaherty failed to live up to his Dad's sterling record.

It seemed to be in his nature [George Bone noted] to be a loser.

Although O'Flaherty's blue 1950s suit was never tatty or shiny with wear, that was your first impression. The young man was neither slack-jawed nor alcoholic, yet your second glance told you he was. And unfortunately for O'Flaherty Gribble, your second glance was almost certain to be your last, if your last had not been your first.

Blundering into things was his forte. As some unfortunates are accident-prone, heaping contusion and injury upon themselves in their hapless stagger through life, O'Flaherty was bad luck–prone.

Like an aberrant human lodestone, he spun his way irresistibly to ill fortune.

The president his father was not pleased. The sainted

gentleman informed O'Flaherty that he had to pull his socks up.

Poor O'Flaherty did not even possess those bizarre or grotesque attributes that mark the neo-Dickensian character as "peculiar, but interesting."

For some, there is a simple joy in giving. For others, an equal joy in taking. O'Flaherty Gribble [as George Bone now began to realize, reviewing this material with a wild growing surmise] was quite lacking in either motive.

When you got down to it, this was the root of O'Flaherty's problem.

He knew neither the smug misery of *doing without*, for which human persons are said to be Saved; nor the pleasing rottenness of *doing*, for which they are held to be Damned.

[George Bone nodded to himself, foreseeing already how this had turned out.]

O'Flaherty Gribble was an Innocent. He had neither Conscience, Shame, nor Guilt.

He dithered through his first year of university (dentistry). He waited for the Last Days but thought it unlikely that any such nonsense would ever come to pass. He helped track down more and more of his ancestral tree, and engaged in mysterious temple rituals for his remote ancestors' postmortem baptism and retroactive salvation, a practice he found touching but dotty.

Against his father's wishes but with his sweet sainted mother's support, he holidayed each year in Sydney at a Gentile uncle's beachside house and learned to love the roar and sparkle and salty crash of the surf.

At the end of his second blundering year of dental science, he wandered away from home and lived in a commune with a group of rejects from the Divine Light Mission. He liked their taste in Eastern music but found their spotty faces rather lifeless.

Irene Branigan dropped in one night in search of an old friend and instead tore O'Flaherty's clothes off under the

influence of boredom and soft drugs. She laughed when
she saw what he was wearing under his suit. She had already laughed at his suit. Still, she was a good-hearted
person, and showed him the way.

They got a flat together, and everyone was very angry.
[George Bone shook his head at this, grimacing.]

O'Flaherty was not fooled, though. This idyllic spell
from the batterings of ill fortune could not last.

He lay one afternoon in the warm breeze of fading summer.

"Come on," Irene cried, bouncing on her knees and
pummelling his chest. "Can't you raise more enthusiasm
than that?" She threatened him with a leather-bound copy
of the *Sutra,* a volume that would have astonished his father.

"Unk. Haven't got the energy."

"You haven't been doing too badly so far, O'Flaherty."

"That's why I haven't got the energy."

"No energy? I've got something here that'll wake you
up, you Mormon backslider." Irene leaped out of bed with
a mad cackle and ran to her huge woollen shoulder bag.

"See if this doesn't pep you up," she told him. In her
hands was the oldest book he'd ever seen.

"I stole it from the Public Library. If they ever catch
me they'll cut off my hands."

As it happens, that was only a joke Irene Branigan was
making. Not until the Interregnum a few years on would
young women routinely have their hands cut off, and then
generally not simply for stealing books but, far worse
crime, for reading them.

O'Flaherty peered over her shoulder. The pages were
ancient and faded and in a kind of pig Latin. He read part
of it aloud, squinting his eyes without his glasses.

"Good God! Do dentists learn Latin these days?"

"I did some in school. Greek too. What's the Qaballah,
anyway?"

"Ancient Jewish mysticism. Get this, my boy—" and

she flung open a page so brilliantly illuminated and dec-
orated that the demon it portrayed seemed to bound from
the vellum right at O'Flaherty's throat.

"The Devil. Gosh, he's fierce."

"It's a recipe," Irene told him, putting her warm hands
on his bare flesh and kneading his ribs. "Let's give the
old boy a call? Hey? Hey? Wadda ya say, O'Flaherty?"

"The *Devil?*" His voice rose incredulously. "Horns and
tail and pitchfork?" He laughed skeptically.

"Aw crap, O'Flaherty. Take a proper look. Where's the
pitchfork?" She flipped the page to another illuminated
letter, this one even more gruesome. "I think Dürer used
this as a model for his engravings."

The monster on the page was all claws and fangs and
steaming snout, incredibly malevolent. O'Flaherty felt
cold, and got up to pull on a sweater.

Irene laughed. "Don't worry, darling," she cried in
delight. "I'm sure this is a foul libel. The Devil is a
smooth, charming gentleman, or would be, if he existed."

[George Bone smiled knowingly to himself.]

O'Flaherty picked out a few more words. He didn't care
for being spooked by some artist's nasty dreams.

"Fortunately there are no difficult ingredients on the list
like wing of the vampire or blood of the newborn babe."
He grinned and cuddled his friend to keep her warm.
"Have you still got some chalk from your teaching
rounds?" She nodded and grinned. "Well, then, let's get
started," and O'Flaherty Gribble gave his first true love a
big juicy smooch, then roared so hard with laughter that
he gave himself hiccups.

They were both terribly taken aback when the crack of
doom exploded across their chalked Triangle of Art and
the candles went out and the air filled up with the choking
pungency of sulphur.

"Shit!" cried Irene Branigan, and passed out.

A dull red glow suffused the room. A tall good-looking

man in the latest continental dinner jacket stood inside the triangle modestly buffing his nails.

O'Flaherty felt slightly put out by the tawdry theatrical effects. He propped Irene on the couch, a preposterously lumpy Brotherhood of Saint Laurence special they'd had the foresight to drag inside their double chalk circles, making room for the Triangle and zodiacal signs and Hebrew and Greek and even more ancient written characters and associated protective pentacles and Stars of David.

"The Devil, I presume."

"At your service."

Flawlessly correct, the Devil returned O'Flaherty's sardonic bow. "You wish, I presume," he said with no beating about the bush, "to sell your soul?"

O'Flaherty needed very urgently to go to the lavatory and had absolutely no intention of leaving the protective circles to do so. Cold sweat poured across his body under his summer clothes. He felt as if somebody big had kicked him in the guts.

Irene was still out cold.

His mind roared into action. Now that he knew he *had* a soul, he had no intention of selling it without having it valued. He fixed the Devil with a fish-cold eye.

"What's the return?"

The Devil raised one eyebrow. "Why, the usual three wishes. I am obliged to stipulate, however, following a little contretemps some decades ago, that the conditions are now slightly more stringent than they used to be, and void if forbidden by State law."

"No paper money?"

"We have no objection to counterfeiting, Mr. Gribble. No, the sorts of rewards withdrawn from offer include physical immortality, unlimited energy, or the total destruction of the world. Interdicted, I'm afraid."

"I see." O'Flaherty paced the inner circumference, thoughtful. This seemed one way to get rid of the bad luck that had jinxed him up to now, or up to meeting Irene, anyway. Unless meeting Irene and her book were the worst of all his rotten luck, and this was going to put the cap on it for good. He made up his mind.

"All right. The soul's yours. What I'd like in return is—"

"One moment, please. We haven't been through the formalities of a valuation." The Devil muttered into his armpit, where something scurried briefly. "I'm having your file sent up together with a Contract Form."

Irene stirred, kicked one leg but failed to waken. O'Flaherty realized that her torpor was probably supernaturally induced. His cold sweat came back. He gritted his teeth and held to his resolve.

A disembodied arm, green and scaly, came down out of the ceiling and handed the Devil a sheaf of papers.

The Devil riffled through them.

His suave smile faded. He frowned. He assumed an arrogant sneer.

"Well, Gribble, it seems you've been wasting my time. You have nothing to sell."

O'Flaherty's nervous elation vanished. He collapsed, nerveless, on the other end of the couch and stared at the Devil with bugged eyes. Mormons are not predestinationists.

"Damned at my tender age? You own my soul already?" The words choked in his throat.

"Your soul?" The Devil looked at him spitefully. "You don't *have* a soul, Mr. Gribble. The idiots sent you down here without one."

"Fasten your seat belts, please, ladies and gentlemen, and extinguish all smoking materials. We are approaching Kingsford Smith airport and should be on the ground in ten minutes. The weather in Sydney tonight is fine, no clouds, and the temperature is still twenty-seven degrees. On behalf of Captain Parry and the rest of the cabin staff, I thank you for flying Australian Airlines, and we hope to enjoy the pleasure of your company again soon. Good evening.''

The plane fell from the black night and across the curved black nothingness of Botany Bay into the lacy glow of Sydney.

"It must have been quite a startling discovery, O'Flaherty," George Bone said.

The astrologer smiled. "Have you ever had occasion to skin an animal, George?"

"I used to be a big-game hunter," Bone reminded him.

"Oh, yes. Well, that's what it was like. Boned. Gutted."

"Quite. I feel for you. My mistake, of course. Never should have happened."

"Don't blame yourself," O'Flaherty told him with a sweet, concerned smile. "Mistakes occur. Nobody's perfect. Well, that is—"

"I'm not sensitive about my shortcomings, son. So what became of you after the Devil turned down your offer?"

"Oh, I drifted about. Dropped dentistry, couldn't stand the bad breath. Eventually I moved over to physics, did a doctorate in stellar dynamics and another one in psychology, a teaching diploma, this and that, picked up a third doctorate in engineering. The usual thing."

"And Irene?"

"Oh. Well, we got married but it didn't last. She never got over seeing the Devil appear in her own lounge room, I suppose. She took up Creation Science, and we more or less drifted apart. Then I fell madly in love with a really beautiful young Greek restaurateur named Spike and made the dumb mistake of taking him home to meet my parents. I mean, George, there I was with a doctorate in *psychology* and I spring from the closet right into my poor old Dad's hands. Spike and I were an item for a while, then I got into the cruising scene and some leather, and eventually AIDS came along and I decided none of it was worth a pinch of salt after all and by then my father had died, so

I moved back in with Mother and concentrated my energies on research.''

"And it's your research that brings you to Sydney?"

Wheels thumped on the tarmac. Engines screamed and shrieked and tried to climb down off the wings, which gave them a shaking for their impertinence.

"Um. The Callisto Effect. I don't suppose you've,'' O'Flaherty started to say out of sheer humble reflex, and then jumped up (having just undone his seat belt) so hard he clouted his head on the plastic overhead locker. "George, tell me! Am I right about the Callisto Effect? Am I going to find a Callisto Prime and validate my theory? You can see into the future, George—grant me this one glimpse. Is Joseph Wagner the man I think he is?"

George Bone stood up and put on his topcoat. He shook his head ruefully.

"I won't tell you things like that, O'Flaherty, and you shouldn't ask me.''

"Oh.'' The astrologer's face fell.

"It would take all the fun out of life if you knew everything in advance, don't you agree?''

"I suppose,'' O'Flaherty agreed reluctantly, following the big man into the arrival lounge. "But if that's so, doesn't it mean astrology and the other psychic sciences're bunkum after all?''

"That's logical, but then consistency has never been my strong point. Well''—Bone held out his hand, and strongly shook O'Flaherty's—"it's been very nice chatting, my boy, and I wish you well in your studies.''

Dazed, O'Flaherty watched him walk briskly away and onto the moving walkway. Somebody stepped forward and took Bone's bag, a uniformed chauffeur by the look of him, and both figures vanished into the crush.

Belatedly, O'Flaherty came to his senses. He dashed after Bone, yelling and waving. People looked at him with disapproval.

"Hey," he called. "Hey, George. What about my *soul?* You never told me what to do about my *soul!*"

But the big man was gone, and O'Flaherty had to mooch gloomily and alone down the escalator to wait by the carousel for his own suitcases to arrive.

chapter fifteen

Seasoned long-distance travellers know there is only one thing worse than waiting at the carousel for your luggage.

This is *giving up* waiting at the carousel because the swine have lost it all between Djakarta and Cairo and you know you'll never see it again.

Hsia Shan-yun, Freda Odell and the rest of the criminals from the shuttle trudged across the vile, open face of the planet Paradise without their luggage, indeed with no possessions whatever except the tatty gowns they wore.

"Essential supplies we can't grow or make for ourselves are dropped in from orbit," a bearded man told Shan, currying favor. Everyone looked at her with a whole lot more respect after her tiff with Anson. "Comes in on 'chutes, no human contact, not even an on-board monitor Bug. Absolutely no machines permitted down here on the surface."

Shan grunted, looking gloomily at the hairy green stuff on the ground and wishing her toes were slurping instead through the foul muck of the dear little brutal cell she'd shared with her close friend Turdington Jimbo.

She felt like crying, but once you've earned a rep as the tough kid on the block you forfeit your right to a good recuperative howl.

The moment of pleasure that had burned like sex through her veins was well behind her. Knowing how to plait a Striped Hole is one thing. Having the raw materials and the time to tangle the threads one over another through ten dimensions in Kaluza-Klein spacetime is another.

"I'm stuck here," she muttered pitifully to herself. "I'll never escape. I'll be a flat-chested dwarf to the end of my days."

In fact, it wasn't until another nine and a half years had dragged by, as measured on Paradise, without any further shuttle-delivered prisoners due to temporary suspension of the program, years of power struggles and attempted rape, of chilly, snow-buried mornings and debilitating forty-five-degree centigrade summer noons, of raising high roof-beams and seeing them crushed by gales of soot, of laughter, somehow, deep and true in the face of adversity, and tears at the loss of loved companions, of getting and spending, remembering and forgetting, taking up the fight and laying down the law, that a passing galactic holiday cruise sponsored by the ladies' auxiliary of the Gamma Globulin combined football leagues landed at the east pole of the convict world Paradise and liberated the pitiful remnants of the prison colony.

The lady lizards' cruise ship, half a million tonnes of squishy lanoline-soaked urdat and runny glass, lingered for an entire month at the delightful east pole, the ladies taking the waters and admiring the views. The bronto-megasaurs of Gamma Globulin, being a race of excessive longevity, never rush their tours.

A party of haggard, desperate human people finally swam, rappeled, white-watered, portaged, and orienteered its frantic way to the plateau where the cruise ship *Snardly Blint* lay crushing a square kilometer of delicious weevil-wart blooms and a few thousand small vertebrates.

Shan-yun, of course, was among the party's number, though on this occasion the rough frontier democratic vote had declined to select her as band leader, which was okay with her. Instead, she was point scout.

"Hey!" she yelled, sighting the cruise ship.

Puffs of smoke were rising from the cruiser's stacks.

A fearful presentiment clutched at her heart.

A weird, ear-hurting mechanical scream was rising from the cruiser's off-side Hyperspatial lifters.

Dazzling beams of multihued elementary particles splattered with motes of exploding photons were rising from the cruiser's pleasure domes.

"Hey, you snotsuckers!" screamed Hsia Shan-yun, running and tripping under the weight of her depleted supply gunnies and handmade fire-hardened machete and bow-and-arrow set.

The cruiser *Snardly Blint* lifted lightly and musically into the frighteningly pellucid sky of Paradise, streamers flying and passengers snug in their acceleration couches.

On board, the captain and her crew played cards and started in on the long drunk that always filled the tedious weeks in Hyperspace between ports of call. None of them—tendrilled, boll-eared, infrared sensitized, locally telepathic—attended to the remote skin microphones that picked up Shan's cries for succour.

This is the way of it with the Bargleplod, a sentient species that has plied the star lanes for upward of seven million years without either taking control of the Milky Way in an outburst of drum-beating imperialism or wiping themselves away in nuclear squabbles.

You'd imagine the Bargleplod would be the envy of everyone, for their relaxed insouciance has guaranteed their survival well beyond the parameters given by Carl Sagan's analysis of interstellar culture. In fact, they're too sloppy and stolid and besotted and dull for anyone sane to envy or emulate.

Hardly surprisingly, it was a Bargleplod who left behind the autonomic mousehunter on the green sweet world Alpha Grommett once was.

Hsia Shan-yun watched incredulously, her enraged, wind-reddened eyes bulging like peeled hard-boiled eggs, as the Bargleplod cruise ship whiffled away into the sky and vanished with an ear-shattering clamor of brute force.

Freda, lithe as a lathe, hardened by adversity, toughened by a history more immediate than any she'd ever subversively programmed into the teaching machines back on Earth, pounded up, breath rasping, and fell against Shan's side.

"Oh shit," she whimpered. "They've gone. They've left us here. We'll never get free now, never, never . . ."

Hsia Shan-yun had been indulging exactly these sentiments, but getting it right in the lughole from a friend she'd trusted to have more gristle got up her nose.

"Come on, Freda, it's not the end of the world. It's just a spaceship flying away. Where there's one visiting alien spaceship there's bound to be another, in a few years, a few decades. Hell, kiddo, we've pulled through this far, haven't we? We've each got five fine kids, and the hospital's almost finished, and if we can get the harvest in before the Big Dry we should see our way to autumn okay. I mean, it's not as if the *sun's* going out or something."

She slapped with by-now-automatic vigilance at her leg.

The animals of Paradise are not always friendly. Anson, for example, had been badly mauled by a wet thing that dropped on his back from a tree and sucked out his brain with an awful slurping noise before anyone could get to it and bash it to death.

Shan gave a cry then, looking down to check on what had tried to bite her.

A small bright machine was casting back and forth blindly through the grass.

It was the first actual, real, metal machine they'd seen on Paradise since their prison shuttle roared away back to orbit.

"Oh! The poor little thing's lost."

"Can it be a—"

"Hubbard's E, Shan, I think it's—"

Shan-yun's hard-boiled eyes bugged with gratitude and pleasure. She started after the cute little scuttling mechanism, brought it to the ground in one practiced pounce, and began to dismantle it.

"An autonomic toaster!"

Freda licked her lips. "If only we had some real sliced bread, the sort they had in the old days back on Earth, came in plastic bags, I can taste that wonderful mold now. If you don't mind my saying, Boss, don't you think it'd function more efficiently if you leave its legs on?"

Shan-Yun sniggered happily.

"Forget the bread, Freda. Don't you see yet what this means?"

Her quite intellectually gifted but less handy colleague's jaw gaped. Blood drained from her cheeks and other places less visible.

"You don't mean . . . ? Surely you can't—"

Shan beamed up at her.

"Yup. With the quark powerpack in this lovely little guy, and a few tufts from its wiring, I'll have a Striped Hole plaited in about three days."

She shot a worried look at the sky. The light was fading, but with any luck she'd have the job well started before dark.

"Watcha got there? Hey, gang, lookit, a *machine!*"

Freda held her finger to her lips, and the arriving party pushed and jostled a bit less noisily, watching the deft weaving fingers of the woman who was about to build them a Hyperspatial wormhole pathway home to Earth and their long-delayed revenge.

chapter sixteen

Sopwith Hammil grated his fire-red Porsche 911 Carrera into the curb and almost struck the sturdy oak trunk thrusting up from a mass of gnarled roots half a meter out from the gutter. The engine died with a refined chortle.

Normally, such a near thing with the trim of his beloved coupe would have caused Sopwith to have a nervy turn. As it was, he'd had his nervy turn back in the comfort and privacy of his own living room and was now 350 degrees into a major nervous breakdown.

He climbed out and slammed the door. In the fading flush of late summer Daylight-Saving twilight, he paused under the heavy green foliage and made himself relax.

The South Yarra apartment Cynthia shared with her old skiing chum Rebel faced the Church of England Girls Grammar School on one side and the Royal Botanic Gardens behind their dark iron-speared fence on the other.

A heady blend of native and introduced floral aromas wafted to Sopwith from the Gardens. It was the perfume of true love and should certainly have been magic to his nostrils.

Sopwith drew a shuddering scented breath and palped his blouson inner pocket for the reassuring box he'd come close to committing mayhem to lay his hands on. The damned jeweller had complained bitterly about opening up on a Sunday night. Thank Christ it hadn't been a Saturday! Sopwith had finally persuaded the fellow only by

virtue of the entrancing prospect of his sparkling craft
splashed in the social pages when the city's foremost television meteor tied the knot under a splash of flashbulbs
and champers.

If Cynthia's apartment had been for auction, the notice
would have said something along these lines:

**A MOST CHARMING ELEVATED FIRST FLOOR
APARTMENT, BEAUTIFULLY SITUATED,
IMMEDIATE VICINITY OF BOTANIC GARDENS,
FEATURES EXCELLENT VIEW OF
CITY SKYLINE**

An entrance hall provides access to a delightfully spacious
combined sitting room and dining room area which opens
to a sun balcony and adjoins a well-equipped kitchen with
eating area. The two bedrooms are also large and cheer-
fully bright. Bathroom and laundry are commodious.
Excellent lock-up garage.
Inspection by appointment.

It was not for auction, however, having been bought for
Cynthia by her daddy on her eighteenth birthday. Lights
showed in its first-floor windows behind the charming
scalloped curtains, lights warm and subdued and welcom-
ing.

Cynthia put up quite well with the constraints of her
lover's live-to-air show and Sopwith wasn't expected for
another half hour, but social niceties were the least of his
worries.

"Soppy!" The brunette—could her name *really* be
Rebel Jasmine Horowitz?—squealed in mock horror, peering through the partly opened door. "Eager tonight, tiger?
Hey, loved your show. Blood and guts, Soppy, blood and
guts, they eat it up."

"Rebel, listen—"

"Come in, don't loiter, man. I'll fix you a drinkie. Cyn's still in the bath, would you believe?"

Sopwith did his best to smile. A deep muffled gonging from a venerable grandfather clock, a Belvue-Bennett heirloom no doubt, set his teeth grinding. Half an hour lost already just getting the bloody ring and making his way here through the stupid bloody one-way streets.

"Thanks, Reb."

"Piña Colada? Kahlúa with vodka? Headbanger?"

"God almighty. Whatever you've got."

"I've got everything you could possibly need, sugar."

"Give me a beer."

"None here. Cyn must have stored it in the kitchen fridge. What can I offer you? Carlton? Fosters? Heineken? Tell you what, Soppy, we've got a darling lager Captain Schauble brought in last week from—"

"A Fosters, Rebel. Just an ordinary bloody Australian Fosters for God's sake."

The woman jerked her head about. "My, we are toey tonight. All that excitement under the hot lights can't be good for you, Soppy. I'm going, I'm going."

The moment her back was turned Sopwith made off on tiptoe for the bathroom.

The flatmate's radar was too good for him. She intercepted him halfway down the hall and wagged a cautionary enamelled fingernail under his nose.

"Naughty, naughty!" She barred his way and bared her pink gums and fabulously expensive teeth. "The poor girl's probably got her face covered with glop. Come back like a good boy and tell Auntie Reb all about that *bitchy* job you did tonight on poor old Freddy—"

Sopwith spun her rudely aside. She bounced against the flocked wallpaper, mouth askew.

"Later, honey. Life and death. Matter of."

Cynthia regarded him with a cool smile as he crashed

into the bathroom and slammed the door behind him. She was quite naked except for one lustrous eyelash.

"My impetuous lover."

"Cyn, there's something—"

"Really, Soppy, sit down there on the loo and take three deep breaths. You look awful."

"Baby!" The pressure was tearing him to shreds. Lungs heaving, he took her advice and sat down on the seat of the lavatory, which bore a still-bright Estapolled decal from an earlier decade of Mick Jagger's lolloping tongue.

Even with her face scrubbed clean and one eyelid twice as heavy as the other, Cynthia Belvue-Bennett was quite surprisingly attractive. Sopwith found that the prospect of sharing a new, primitive world with her, in the company of a select group of superior survivors, while hardly as pleasing as his continued exposure every Sunday night to millions of enthralled and admiring viewers, was not without its appeal. He let these insights coagulate slowly through his mind while he got his voice back into working order.

"I couldn't wait," he said rather flaccidly.

"You'll have to, lover. We don't have time, even if you are here half an hour early."

"Cynthia, I—I want to marry you, Cyn."

The eyelash jumped off Cynthia's face and lowered itself to the ground like a spider.

The eye proper widened, as did its colleague, with joy and amazement. Cynthia flung herself into Sopwith's arms, banging her knees on the bathroom tiles.

Like many of her peers, Cynthia Belvue-Bennett was living proof of the theory of thirty-year cycles. Having missed out on the fifties and the twenties, she was doing it all anyway, with due allowance for the benefits of contraception and jet transport.

"Darling! How romantic! Nobody's asked me to marry them in *months!*"

"Is that a yes or a no?"

"Father will be cross, of course. The old fart's had his heart set on a baronet, at least. I keep telling him that if he wants a baronet he's going to have to set me up in Sloane Square, but then he's never been very—"

"Cynthia, *are you going to marry me or not?*"

"—bound to give in gracefully after a month or two of cajoling." She smothered his face with a mouth tasting of fluoride toothpaste, whirled away, caught up a frilly *peignoir*. "Golly, Reb'll be so excited. What a wedding we'll have . . . St John's, all the TV channels, everyone who's any—"

Sopwith seized her cruelly by the shoulders and shook her rather a lot.

Gone for one heavenly moment, the gruesome droning pressure was back, squeezing his brain, pounding on the top of his eyeballs, churning in his tummy.

"Don't understand, Cynthia. No wedding. No time for that."

She pulled away with the strength and balance of a seasoned skier.

"No *wedding*? Sopwith Hammil, what are you—"

"Nothing *elaborate* is what I mean," he cried in a strangled voice. "The sun. Turned off, don't you understand? We have to get married tonight."

"*Tonight?*"

"Right away, baby. Take that silly thing off and get some clothes on, and we'll—" He was pulling her toward the bathroom door as she was clinging to the basin, one leg hooked under the lavatory bowl.

"That's just plain ridiculous, Sopwith. Mother and I have been planning my wedding for years. Besides, you can't just *get married*. This isn't Reno, you know. There are bans, people have to be notified, for heaven's sake, though it is sweet of you, Soppy, you impetuous fool, come here and let me—"

"I've made the arrangements. Know people in high places, have to in my job, a touch of pressure on the nerve.

Don't think it was easy, Cyn, not on a Sunday night, my God, but I've bribed a clerk in the Registry Office to backdate the forms and they're opening a side room in the—"

"Are you *on drugs,* Sopwith? Have you been taking those little blue pills again? Bribed? Registry Office?" She lunged for the door, got past his blocking shoulder, ran into the hall.

"We can be legally married inside an hour," Sopwith shrieked at her. "Don't you understand? I'm doing this for both of us!"

"The most important day in my life and you try to throw mud on it! You brute. Get out! Go on, piss off. You're a *kink,* that's what you are. A sadist. I should have guessed when you brought that bondage kit around last—"

"That was just something I read about in *Penthouse,*" Sopwith sobbed. He looked at his digital watch. Two hours remaining. She saw him look at his watch and her face changed from suspicion to rage. He was forced to back away from her fury, mumbling, attempting to explain the inexplicable. "If you'll just let me—"

A profound, sickening conviction rose within him, as it does within the heart and soul of everyone who has ever tried to convey an impossibly difficult truth (such as, for example, the Kaluza-Klein theory of superstrings in ten-dimensional space with suppression of six of the dimensions to make the theory compatible with Einstein's general relativity while retaining unification of bosonic and hadronic particles at the field level), that he should never have started this conversation.

Perhaps he ought to have begun at the beginning and told her the unvarnished truth.

No. At any rate, he couldn't do so at this point. She'd never accept it, except as the bleatings of a lunatic.

One small part of his consciousness watched Rebel Jasmine Horowitz watching him being pushed down the hall by his maddened lover. A liquid gleam of sexual interest shone in her dark eye.

He was shoved bodily out the front door onto the private first-floor landing. Even as the door slammed in his face, Cynthia got in the last word.

"You don't need a wife, you monster. You need a *psychiatrist!*"

He crouched on the landing in silence for ten minutes. The world whirled.

Maybe he *was* going crazy. No, that was crazy. He'd seen that damned ugly thing from the future, seen it appear as a loaf of bread in the middle of his sofa, seen it turn into a disgusting chitinous insect, seen it vanish quite away.

If it had given him three hours to get back, legally mated and with documentation to that effect stamped and in hand, it meant what it said.

Could he fake it?

Sopwith shuddered, and hunkered down, hugging his knees into his forehead. No way. The insect would *know*. It was that sort of insect.

Sopwith stood up.

He turned around and knocked firmly on the door.

After a palpable pause, it opened a crack.

Sopwith placed his bloodshot eye close to the crack.

"Cynthia," he whispered hoarsely.

"Beg my forgiveness for your horrible behavior," Cynthia said. She had been crying, he saw, and was now coldly seething. "Crawl to me on your hands and knees."

"Cynthia," Sopwith said. "You don't believe me, I know, but for pity's sake try. Please try. Some creatures from the future are going to turn the sun off tonight. I can help you escape to another era. Will you come down now with me to the Registry Office and get married?"

The door slammed in his face, slightly bruising his right cheekbone.

After a while another idea came to him.

He knocked firmly on the door.

After a palpable pause, Rebel Jasmine Horowitz opened it a crack.

Sopwith placed his bloodshot eye close to the crack.

"Rebel," he whispered hoarsely.

"You rat," Rebel told him in a low, sexy whisper.

"Rebel," Sopwith said. "Rebel, will you marry me?"

The door slammed in his face, badly bruising his right cheekbone.

chapter seventeen

What Sopwith needed and had no time to seek out was the advice of an ace Heart-Balm columnist.

The finest Heart-Balm columnist in the universe was, at that very moment, examining her modem-linked terminal's bulletin board.

The day's dreadful temperatures had dropped only a little, but inside her steamy, climate-set module on Alpha Grommett the stout green lizard known to millions of *Intelligencer* readers as Meg Kindheart fanned herself with her claw more for metaphoric narrative purposes than because she was genuinely overheated, and crossed the room from her escritoire to draw the mica curtains.

Halfway through her first millennium, Mrs. Emilia Aardwimble had retired from her position as Matron of Eggs after a massive cholesterol-induced heart attack—a leading cause of fatalities in brontomegasaurs because of the tremendous strain any big dino species has just got to suffer living out of water—followed by intermittent but troubling cardiac troubles.

Casting about for an interest, she chanced during a long recuperative galactic tour upon the unusual machine city of Rock-Breaks-Scissors, with which for reasons not even she could explain she fell instantly in love.

Perhaps it was the boom and clack, the humming industry.

Perhaps it was the strange beauty of an entire planet

unrestricted by the ecological niceties of organic life, so that poisonous but lovely fumes gusted ceaselessly across a sky like beaten egg-yolk (though this was scarcely an image Mrs. Aardwimble would have permitted to linger within her conscious awareness) and delirious young mechanisms sported merrily in mineral tailings so carcinogenic they'd instantly bring cancers boiling through the lung and digestive tract of any unprotected creature based on the carbon molecule.

Now, for a moment, Mrs. Aardwimble stood at her triple-sealed window, gazing at the flaring yellow sky and the viridescent angular shapes of the city.

A breezy tornado came off the liquid mercury sea, raising a purple haze, carrying to her ears through the sturdy walls of her life-support module the happy bleats and pitterings of machines at play.

Emilia smiled to see their happiness, but her smile grew wistful as she remembered the thousands who did not share it.

Slowly, she turned her great green mass, pivoting solemnly on her tail, and made her way back to her screen's index of tragic letters.

Most of these communications were too intimate and shocking to answer through the newspaper. Meg Kindheart always sent personal replies to these letters, direct, via the Ethernet. It was her most appealing and pumppriming feature, yet most of her readers were quite unaware of it.

She sat down in the huge hydraulic chair with the slot cut for her tail, glancing, as she always did, at the umber hologram of her four hatchlings and the more recent deepimage holos of the grandchildren. As reptiles, her species on Gamma Globulin bred slowly, but they bred surely.

Fervently, Mrs. Emilia Aardwimble thanked the Great Whistling Moon that the kids had grown up healthy, strong and happy. If only—

Young Brian Aardwimble's face smiled poignantly from one of the earliest of the holograms, breaking her heart.

Brian, the brilliant saurian musician, the master of contrapuntal warbling, the prodigy who had died so tragically young.

Only Mrs. Aardwimble and her inseminator knew that Brian had farned himself in an arkle.

Only they knew the anguish of their mistakes, of forcing him in the egg, of demands imposed in the long dreaming years within its leathery shell, years that ought to have been a period of prebirth meditation and tranquillity but which they had made a nightmare of competitive pressure and premature peer rivalry.

Yet out of suffering, she knew, gazing at his young likeness, comes a measure of wisdom.

Sighing, Mrs. Aardwimble called up the first pleading cry for help.

The letter was from a young mechanism, already in the throes of replication after a thoughtless bout of solitary self-loodling, driven to distraction by its predicament. It was thinking of erasing its ROM chip.

With a wrench, Mrs. Aardwimble looked again at Brian's portrait, and away. Carefully, choosing her words with precision, she wrote a message of solace to the pregnant machine.

It would not appear in the *Intelligencer*. This was a personal lifeline, a work of organic love.

No machine would have dreamed of doing such a thing.

Because no machine would dream of doing such a thing was precisely *why* the world of Alpha Grommett needed Mrs. Emilia Aardwimble, or some living creature like her.

The next letter was from an ageing housebot, a rather silly, selfish mech who wanted all the answers without any of the effort. She at least had a dream, one she wished Meg Kindheart to endorse, but it was a heedless, feckless dream.

She sought approval to leave her spouse and escape with some shining hero of fantasy.

Her name, as you will have guessed, was Sally Diode.

The big lizard eased her buttocks and put her snout into her cupped claws. Her compassion was tinged with disgust. Uncertain of how best to reply, she returned the letter to its holding register.

Thirteen letters down the stack she came on another, which might have been the mirror image of Mrs. Diode's.

It began sarcastically, even rudely. Mrs. Aardwimble was tempted to ZAP it, but hesitated because of an element of loss, of frustration behind the bitterness.

The machine that had input these words was disappointed with marriage, with his career, with everything. The final challenge was ironic, but Mrs. Aardwimble responded to the unhappy aspiration beneath it:

"Do you suggest, Miss Heal-All Kindfart, that I should leave my little brood and seek a True Love in the great wide world?"

The letter, yes, was from Bruce Diode.

Mrs. Emilia Aardwimble was not without a deeply compassionate sense of humor. Smiling broadly, she called the earlier letter into an adjacent window and sat considering her replies.

chapter eighteen

"You're sure it won't blow up on us?"

"Of course I'm sure. Hold that light steady."

"It'd make a terrible mess."

Shan-yun said nothing, squinting through her scratched-out corneas at the wobbling skein of energy. She licked her lips and pushed another string into the blistered surface.

"I mean, that's what you were sent here for, isn't it? Trying to blow everything up."

Shan blew up.

"Listen, I've been working two centimeters from this singularity for five days now and my patience is just about worn right through, so if you want to *walk* home, you squawking, blathering, onion-breathed, interfering—"

"All right, all right." The felon backed away from the fire, muttering and scowling sullenly. "Just don't blame me, tooter," Shan-yun thought she heard him start to add, but there was nothing she could do about leaping up and boxing his ears for him because if she let go of the almost-completed Striped Hole everything really *might* blow.

Freda said quietly in her ear, "How long now?"

"Dunno. Couple of minutes."

"I'll get everyone formed up."

The children were pushed into line, thin and scrawny, in handwoven clothing that would certainly draw unfavorable attention when they suddenly materialized back inside some part of the State on Earth.

Still, their prospects were better on the home world than here, because for the first time in some dozen decades there was going to be gathered in one place an entire community of rebels, people who'd come through the fire and been tempered in it, people who knew how to work and plan and survive together against all odds.

The tip of Shan-yun's tongue protruded from the corner of her mouth as she slotted the final superstring into place.

Like a blue ball of charged plasma, the Striped Hole hung in the air beside the camp fire. It was an extrusion into human-perceivable spacetime from a higher realm, and in minutes everyone on the planet Paradise was going to step into its insane Hyperspatial wormhole and plunge infinitely faster than light, along its slippery slide, back to Earth.

"I'm not going," old Harry suddenly declared in his mulish way. "Won't get me into one of them damn fangled contraptions."

Before panic could spread, Shan-yun beckoned the old-timer close and leaned toward his ear. As he bent to her, she tripped him and sent him across her shoulder in a perfect judo fall.

Harry struck the seething surface of the Hole and dopplered in so fast not even his scream of protest got away.

"Works okay," Shan muttered darkly.

There was a belated round of applause, and she was borne about the camp fire on everyone's shoulders. Before they could break out the last of the wart-wine for a celebration binge, she kicked and wriggled back to her feet and hollered for attention.

"I can't guarantee the stability of this mock-up. We have to follow Harry right now."

A ripple of fear rippled fearfully through the frightened gathering.

"I'll lead the way," resolute Freda said before they could all get out of control.

She stepped forward, holding one hand in a careless gesture under her chin to stop her teeth chattering. "Come on, kids, last one in's a jumbled genotype!"

The Striped Hole gulped her down without a belch.

One by one the pitiful remnants of the prison planet stepped forward and took their dive.

When the last one was gone Hsia Shan-yun looked about with bittersweet happy sadness at the world that had been all of freedom to them, and all of hell too.

Were they right in abandoning this frontier world where they owned a kind of artless liberty?

Might they bring salvation from oppression to their brothers and sisters on Earth?

Or would the invincible robot Bugs be waiting, ready to ensnare them in projected gloop the moment they materialized?

The cold night air brought only strange unearthly odors and no answers!

Wiping away a tear, Shan put out the last fire on the planet Paradise, raked the hot cinders over with dirt, and stepped into the Striped Hole, pulling it shut behind her.

She had forgotten the side effects from the Hyperspatial implants the State's medics had put inside her.

Hideous forces screeched through the ten dimensions of Kaluza-Klein high space.

Hadronic fields uncurled and punched bosonic fields in the throat.

Massless particles got heavy, heaving their way sluggishly through the void and saying rude words to anyone they met.

For Shan-yun, it felt like a clumsy nurse taking sutures out of a razored eyeball that hasn't quite healed.

It felt like a car running you down, starting with your feet and moving slowly but surely toward your skull.

It felt like finding you've missed the math exam because you thought it was on the next day.

It felt, in fact, unspeakably worse than all these things, because as the space dimensions curled up from the unprecedented shock of an Immovable Object meeting an Irresistible Force and the time dimensions unrolled, throwing Shan-yun backward into history instead of sideways across the light-years back to Earth, she understood something that made her howl with remorse.

She understood that with a slight twist here and a minor bend there she could have used her Striped Hole to unzip the Hyperspatial Restructurators embedded within her deformed body and set free her original form.

It was like finding that you tore up your winning million-dollar lottery ticket.

It was like tearing up the rest of your life.

"Excuse me, dearie, are you all right?"

She found that she was sitting in the back of a large hall where a bizarre gathering of primitive male and female human people were milling aimlessly, chattering without any point to it, leaning forward on seats staring at the floor and trying not to be sick, coming forward to the brightly lit front of the hall when their names were called, laughing on cue when the lights flashed in a big cheery endless loop around the sign reading: *!!!THE NEW PERFECT MATCH!!!*

"Uh, whaaa—?"

"You look as if you could do with a nice cup of tea, dear. Look, the canteen's just down the corridor outside the red door, why don't we nip out and have a cuppa and a Bex. It's the spotlights and the noise, that's all. Goodness, what an unusual dress. Is that from Myers?"

Shan-yun took her bitten hands out of her mouth and looked from the kindly cleaning woman who stood patting her shoulder to the made-up secondhand car salesmen and blowsy blondes with sun-reddened shoulders sticking out of the tops of their flounced dresses and toothy potato-faced wholesale butchers talking about yachts and giggling hairdressers with bright fingernail polish and a jumping enthusiast who seemed to be orchestrating the entire procedure with buzzers sounding and big slides flashing on and off and people with earphones pushing and pulling enormous machines that could only be primitive picture-transmitting equipment.

The woman had spoken to her in a kind of English, which of course she knew from her old forbidden books and tapes.

"A cuppa," she said experimentally. "How nice. I would be delighted. Lay on, MacDuff."

The red-cheeked woman laughed gaily. "There, you're sounding more chipper already. Come on, then, we might be able to get a cream bun if that guts Marge hasn't scoffed the lot."

Fortunately Shan's new friend had some of the metal tokens that were needed in exchange for services in this time frame, and was kind enough to offer the serving person some of them on Shan's behalf.

They chatted across a table covered by some hard shell filled with glittering specks of mica, and the nice lady asked Shan's name and Shan remembered a book she'd read from this time period about a great mathematician and she remembered also a lovely woman who'd been in a film about politicians and she decided prudence was safer than time paradoxes, although it was rapidly dawning on her that a good macro-paradox was probably the only way she would ever attract enough attention to allow her to get her hands on the makings for another Striped Hole so she could use it to unzip her filthy stinking unfair rotten Hyperspatially Restructurated implants and get home to her kids.

"There, that's put the color back into your cheeks," the kind woman said. "I'll leave you find your own way back, dear," she added, popping a striped scarf back on her very strangely colored hair, and went back to her mops and buckets while Hsia Shan-yun began to prowl up and down the corridors of the big echoing building until another woman, thin and elegant and disdainful, caught her by the arm.

"In here, you've been past twice already, can't you read?"

"I can read very well," Shan said proudly, taking a seat in front of the disdainful woman's desk as she was instructed to do.

"I don't seem to have your name here. They sent you up from the front office?"

"I found my own way," Shan said.

"Hmmph," the woman told her. "Well, what's your name?"

"Mariette Planck," said Hsia Shan-yun with a delicious sense of anticipation.

"I'll see if Sopwith can fit you in now," the woman said angrily. "They really should have your name on the list, it's extremely aggravating."

chapter nineteen

"The evidence is abundant," cried ebullient O'Flaherty Gribble, perched on Joe Wagner's desk. The surface of the desk was littered with clean, practiced diagrams which O'Flaherty scattered from his Texta without pausing in his headlong spruiking.

"But where's the *theory* in all this?" Joe complained.

Across the room, the monkeys were babbling excitedly and shaking at their grilles. For a gleeful moment he imagined they were responding after all to some pheromone from Fat Mac, but when he took a close look it was evident that O'Flaherty's mania was the sole responsible agency.

Perhaps I should remind you that during this time frame, human people by and large fell into one of only two major categories.

Most were pitifully credulous.

A few, generally those with intellectual training, were pitifully incredulous.

You could take a representative of the first group and tell him that by rubbing the well-used seat of an old bicycle over his navel he might rid himself of lung cancer and within a week no cyclist in the land would dare leave his machine unattended.

Of course, even this broadly valid rule possessed some important exceptions.

You could, for example, tell the same credulous fellow that smoking cigarettes would *give* him cancer, and he'd laugh in your face, coughing and wheezing while he did it.

Still, the generalization holds. Bracing, well-defended incredulity was almost wholly reserved to the ranks of those trained like mazed rats in the doctrines of their mentors.

Incredulity was not by any means a bad thing, however. You can't have the creative people in a community going about just *believing* things at random.

It's perfectly safe to let the donkeys and drudges believe to their hearts' content. It keeps them fairly quiet and dispels any envy that might creep into their souls at the sight of those few who've escaped to a life not entirely mindless and inertial.

Joe Wagner hardly saw himself as rigid, unimaginative, shackled by the Ontological Consensus of his fellow scientists and industrial artisans. Even so, he wasn't going to sit still for this arrant nonsense.

"First you get a mathematical theory," he told O'Flaherty patiently. "Then you see what it predicts. That's the hard part. And afterwards you go looking at the world to see if your prediction's right. Isolated facts are quite meaningless. They're like isolated grains of sand—useful for building sand castles with."

"I see that you haven't built many sand castles," O'Flaherty cried in frustration. "You need a lot of wet sand firmly packed together. Aren't you listening? This is my theory—well, the celebrated Gauquelin's theory, actually: that a significantly greater proportion of distinguished people will be born just after the rise or culmination of certain planets."

" 'Culmination'?"

"When the planet is directly overhead."

"That's not a theory," Joe said in disgust. "That's a crackpot assertion. I want some differential equations."

"You won't get them because it's too soon for that sort of model-building," O'Flaherty said. "Isn't it enough to know that between two and four percent more babies than you'd expect by chance born at the rise or culmination of Mars and Jupiter become important military figures and sports champions and politicians? That the same excess is found among writers in relation to the rising and culmination of the Moon?"

"Two or three percent? A statistical fluke, O'Flaherty, absolutely meaningless. You've been staring through your damned horoscope so long you've grown hairs on your eyeballs."

O'Flaherty took no offense. He sighed and flung down his felt pen.

"Joe, I sought you out at great cost and effort, I came here today, because and only because my theory predicted quite firmly that something unprecedented would have happened in your life. Grant me that."

The biochemist looked moodily at his shoes. They needed a shine.

"Say that sort of thing to anyone and they'll find some interesting story to tell. Purely psychological."

"The massed Salvation Army Women's Band forcing you to jump out of the top deck of a moving bus? Really, Joe, let's have some intellectual rigor and honesty here."

"All right, I admit that's a bit strange—"

"You were in tears of frustration when I got in here."

"—but I certainly haven't begun to exhaust the natural explanations yet."

"Would you like me to open the door and call Enid in?"

Joe looked up in alarm.

"Don't you dare! Oh, very well, of course I think it's pretty strange, you turning up when you did. But you could have been on the bus, for all I know. You could have followed me here in another cab and hung about until you got my name and then burst in here with your crazy—"

He trailed off, feeling foolish and paranoiac and unfairly put-upon.

"But I didn't do any of those things," O'Flaherty said gently. "I know who you are because I've run all the birth registration records for the past sixty-three years through a computer search . . ."

"That's supposed to be privileged information," Joe mumbled.

"I'm associated with several Life Assurance corporations, Joe. If you want to see real magic at work, watch the doors open when you've one of those guys backing you."

"I still think it's unethical."

O'Flaherty rubbed his nose and then took off his glasses and rubbed them as well.

"What harm can I do? If the Callisto Effect is confirmed, I've launched a new science. Otherwise the thing is disproved, and I've done people of your particular faith a signal service by hammering another nail into the coffin of superstition. No?"

"Well, you're pestering me now, aren't you, and taking up valuable research time. That's a kind of harm, isn't it?"

O'Flaherty rose at once and moved to the door.

"If you wish me to leave, Joe, naturally I'll leave you in peace. I thought you'd jump at the chance to find out what's happened to you."

A vision scrambled through Joe's battered brain with all the careless unconcern for his feelings which Fat Mac would show, searching his thinning hair for nits.

Women.

Strange women with staring, lustful eyes.

"This is silly," he said. "Here, sit down. Can I get you a cup of instant?"

"Never drink it," O'Flaherty said apologetically. "It

disturbs the vibrations. No, don't hit me, just joking," he cried, laughing like a drain.

I could spend pages telling you in painful detail the nature of O'Flaherty Gribble's hypothesis, but if you want to know about it you can read Michel Gauquelin's book *Cosmic Influences on Human Behavior,* or the skeptical pop sci treatment of astrology by Professor Hans Eysenck and D. K. B. Nias, which much to their own horror endorses Gauquelin's statistics and methodology.

Being neither credulous nor incredulous myself I will reserve my own verdict.

The essence is this: Gauquelin (and O'Flaherty after him) claimed a link between major success in human endeavor and the celestial position of certain planets of the solar system. When the moon Callisto was incorporated into this set of correlations, an extraordinary result fell out of the numbers.

"Callisto Prime!" O'Flaherty said with a return of unchecked enthusiasm.

"You're telling me that forty-two years ago I was born between the appearance of Callisto over the horizon and the rising of Jupiter sixty-six seconds later?"

"So I surmise from the effect you are having on women today."

"Why this particular birthday?"

"Maybe it's the number forty-two, which keeps cropping up for some reason."

"Give me a break."

"No, mostly it's because the planets achieved a curious alignment at about eleven o'clock last night, all favorable for you."

"Just for me, eh? Me and good dead Don Juan."

"For *any* potential Callisto Prime anywhere in the world—but I think you're probably the only one. The odds are vanishingly small."

"Jupiter, Saturn, Mars, Venus, and Callisto, eh?"

"No, Callisto and Ganymede have no significant influence in the present ignition sequence. Only the major planets. You neglected the Moon, by the way."

"The Moon's not a bloody *planet,*" Joe shouted. "It's a *moon.*"

"Astronomical realities are not strictly relevant, Joe, surely you see that. We're dealing with a mixture of symbols and primary forces."

Joe felt himself choking. "Suppose I accept this madness provisionally. How would such favor manifest itself?"

"Why, in the first instance, through the benefits of love. All right, don't get excited, I know that's shamelessly unscientific. Call it 'compulsive projective erototropism' if it makes you feel better. Call it 'cerebrosexual osmosis.' "

"Snide bugger."

"Venus supplies the motif of sexual arousal, Jupiter of masculine conquest," O'Flaherty said blithely, "while Saturn as the father of Jupiter intensifies these aspects to the magnitude of a Prime."

"Gibberish. I can't stand it. What about the bloody Moon?"

"Ah, there we have the key to the next stage in the unfolding of your prodigious talents." O'Flaherty glanced at his watch. "Something I've always hoped to witness and never dared to expect."

Joe Wagner was aghast.

"There's *more?* More than all the women up and down the street baying for my blood?"

"Hardly your *blood,* Joe."

O'Flaherty batted his eyelashes saucily, and for the first time the biochemist realized his curious visitor was gay. It made him uncomfortable; he had never been altogether at ease with homosexuality, although he professed a suit-

able liberal approval of its unfettered practice among the
pitiful weirdos of that persuasion.

"Well, no. Still."

"The blatant Orphean sexual aspects are purely super-
ficial, Joe. I wouldn't be surprised if they've lost their
compulsive force already."

Joe's face fell. Frightening and distasteful as the experience had been, he had come rather to relish the prospects
of his charisma.

O'Flaherty smiled hugely and clapped him on the shoulder.

"Fear not, Joe, it's still there, I'm sure—only under
better control. Like an adolescent breaking his voice in,
braying all over the place until it settles down. You should
be safe enough on the bus home."

"I think I'll phone for a taxi anyway." He considered
opening the door and testing O'Flaherty's hunch with
Enid, but shrank from so hazardous a proof. "Well, what's
this famous 'next stage'?"

O'Flaherty gazed at him with a look of such tenderness
that Joe's testicles snapped up against his buttocks and
quivered there.

"Direct sympathetic coercion of energy fields, Joseph," O'Flaherty said reverently.

"What? What? No, don't say it again, I couldn't stand
it."

"I think I can teach you to reach right inside the sun
and divert gravitational energy at your command."

Joe's face went utterly white.

His teeth felt as if they had been extracted and thrown
away to die.

He believed O'Flaherty with all his heart and soul.

"The sun? Are you *insane?* Pull a bit of the *sun* inside
this room?"

"In controlled form," O'Flaherty hastened to stress,
his dexterous right hand sketching again, diagrams and
symbols and flow charts which drew in Joe's eye and then

his brain until the spirit of the daylight-hidden Moon swelled in his breast and he heard its echo within him, like Earth to sun, Moon to Earth, anode to cathode, link to link.

"That's one of your blessed Striped Holes, isn't it?"

"I'm glad somebody pays attention to Sopwith Hammil's program."

"You want me to *build* a Striped Hole, O'Flaherty?"

"You can do it, I'm sure. Like falling off a log."

So Joe Wagner put his hand into the middle of the sun and pulled out a plum, a fat red juicy plum of ten spinning maddened dimensions, and set it in the air and watched it seethe while O'Flaherty Gribble felt tears running down his face as everything his life had ever been came together in this one glorious, unbearable moment of joy.

With a tremendous bang of wind that slapped them both across the room, the Striped Hole vanished into nowhere and the door of the lab burst inwards and shatterproof glass from the windows shivered and blasted the room with dust.

Enid rushed into the room and helped them to their feet.

Fat Mac screamed with delight and clapped his little black hands together.

Joe Wagner, biochemist and thaumaturgist, shook his head in amazement.

"Right." He looked hard at O'Flaherty. "Now I suppose you'll want to see that again in slow motion."

They began to pummel each other like boisterous boys, while Enid watched them with pained disapproval.

Thaumaturgist? It's been worrying you, I know. Old Greek religious word. *Wonderworker.*

chapter twenty

The sky over Rock-Breaks-Scissors was deep violet, tinged with a gray deep enough to be edible.

Bruce Diode leaned back against the leaf-spring shock absorbers of his traction line, zipping home. The volcanoes had brought dreadful weather the past few weeks. High above the carbon dioxide atmosphere, clouds of sulphuric acid swept across the countryside, pouring down as dreary corrosive rain each night and ruining the children's outdoor games.

Still, despite the humidity, the weather did seem to be clearing up.

Bruce was, frankly, more relaxed and at ease with himself than he'd been for years, though his cabinet tingled and surged with excited expectation. He hadn't felt this way since his courtship, and even that had been a rigid, controlled business.

Eagerly, Mr. Diode anticipated the joys of getting home from work.

The snaking line of robots clipping on and off the traction, almost alive in the gloom, came to a ragged halt at an earthquake fracture. While the autonomics spurted out their quick-setting crystal bridgework, Bruce jounced impatiently against his springs.

At length, unable to wait until he got home to the privacy of his study, he rolled his eyes inside his cabinet and called up the latest letter from his secret sweetheart.

"My darling," ran the words across his inward screen, "I cannot imagine how I lived before we met. But that's silly, isn't it?—because we have not met. Or perhaps we have, perhaps our chips were etched by the same Xaser, doped from the same source, and perhaps in these bytes we take from each other, a link has been forged between two wild spirits."

Something strange was happening to his sensors, or to the interpretive matrix that took in the data from his sensors.

The copper greens of the buildings nearby shimmered with light even though the sun was setting.

Bruce Diode shivered, too, with besotted love.

"I like to believe that we are the only two of our model, stamped out as a pair, the mold broken. O my love, my yet-nameless love, can we not go together into that world of our dreams where I see you now only during off-peak inactivation? Impossible? I cannot believe it . . ."

Tenderly, Bruce sent the magic bits back to enciphered safekeeping.

A splatter of drops fell, and the traction system raised its perfunctory shields. Bruce felt like crying aloud with bittersweet rejoicing.

"Rain," his lover had written, "how like the pain which falls in cruel droplets when love is lost. If only my spouse could understand—"

Well, Bruce growled to himself, *damn* the big dumb insensitive brute.

And so on.

"You'll understand," Meg Kindheart had written to him, "why I cannot publish this letter. But I see a way to help you find yourself. Are you married to the wrong kind of mechanism? Why, then, let me introduce you to a 'bot suffering the same agonies, a sensitive dreamer, someone you might love if only I can bring you together."

Bless her, he thought.

The traction released him. The rain had stopped, but there were no activity signals coming from his home.

All the better.

He rolled in, plittered up and down the inquiry band. Nobody answered. Sally was out visiting one of her vapid friends and he'd have to make do with the leavings from the morning sump.

One light burned in his study, on the bulletin board. He rolled forward on his fat little wheels, extensors quivering, and jacked in.

It was not from his lover. Disappointment crushed him briefly, to be replaced by new excitement. It was a note from Meg Kindheart.

An invitation to Scissors Heights! For dinner! This very evening!

Bruce felt his intelletron whir. The intimation was clear. His beloved would be there.

Zealously, he scrubbed down his cabinet and polished his lenses. Scampering like a young mech, he dashed for the outbound traction and plugged in.

Bald wheels spinning free, he plunged toward his destiny.

There's no point in laboring this, I trust?

Yes, the big elegantly dressed lizard met Bruce at the door.

Yes, he was led in to the steamy, somewhat uncomfortable living room.

Yes, he found himself staring at a large worn Art Deco radio, whom he saved from pitching on its dial with a deft sweep of his extensor.

Yes, he tweetered like a fool and radiated all over the place while Mrs. Amilia Aardwimble lumbered graciously from the room.

"Poor Sally," Bruce Diode thought, when he was capable of thinking the next thing. "She looks as if she will die of mortification."

Then he saw himself clearly, abandoning embarrassment, forgetting pettiness, seeing as well, before him, the mechanism that had written those glorious, those gorgeous letters.

The 'bot he had never really known!

And somehow he knew deep within his most hard-wired circuits that Sally was seeing him in the same perspective, as the shining servomech of his letters to her, the passionate machine that until now had always been afraid to cry out its wonder and joy—and, he thought, all aglow with joy and wonder, his love, his *love*.

With tremendous dignity, utterly sure of himself at last, Bruce Diode rolled across the floor and placed his wife's trembling lateral extensor against the side of his ingestion orifice.

And Sally looked back at him and she saw a little funny machine like a Singer Sewer with bits added on by Gyro Gearloose, and she forgave him the endless irritations, the selfishness, the private detective paperbacks, the humorless pedestrian dreariness of him, and saw too that he was her great and shining hero at last.

Machines don't laugh, though, which is a terrible shame.

For if these two had been human people and by some miracle they hadn't already slaughtered each other with any heavy instrument that happened to be lying conveniently to hand or run fuming from the room in the very first enraged moment, why, then they'd have leaned on each other's necks and laughed together, laughed and roared and guffawed and groaned with the outrage of it until tears ran down their cheeks.

But robots never laugh, so instead Bruce and Sally Diode bowed in a dignified fashion to each other and, extensors linked, rolled together in pursuit of Mrs. Emilia Aardwimble and their promised dinner.

For Sopwith Hammil, I regret to say, marriage took quite a different course.

chapter twenty-one

The dash clock blipped its message of unstoppable, creeping doom.

Sopwith Hammil stared at the crimson numerals with eyes of a similar hue. Less than an hour and a half left. His knuckles cracked.

"Oh God," he groaned in a heartfelt soliloquy that travelled straight to George Bone's inward ear, was heard, noted, filed, and acted upon only with the most refined and metaphysical indirection.

"Oh God, I've taken at least a hundred of the nation's most desirable women into my bed in the past two years alone, and I can't think of one who'd marry me on an hour's notice."

Worse, he couldn't help thinking of the gloating TV magazine writers who drooled ceaselessly on his behalf over the hordes of women who watched him every Sunday night, each of them, it was said, frantic to share his sheets.

"Where are you now," he cried aloud, "when I need you?"

Probably he could drive to St. Kilda and do a deal with a hooker past her prime, or find some pathetic smacked-out wretch so sunk in stupor she'd go along with anything.

The idea made him shudder. As a line of thought it was simply too gruesome to pursue. He'd rather be dead, literally, than be forced to spend the remainder of his life marooned with a slag like that in some alien epoch.

One thing was dead clear—there was certainly no point in rushing like a lunatic from one cafe society apartment to the next, proposing wedlock to erstwhile bed partners in the remote hope of finding one who'd deem it more than a gag in poor taste. He'd come to grief before at the hands of the bush-telegraph operated by Cynthia and her chums.

Doubtless Cyn or Rebel or Cyn *and* Rebel were on the phone at this very minute, relating in awful and increasingly inventive detail exactly what kind of weirdo freakout shit Sopwith Hammil had proved to be.

He found himself panting noisily like a perspiring German short-haired pointer. "My mind's shot to ribbons," he muttered. He hunched over the leather-wrapped wheel. "I need advice." What he needed, he saw, was a cool, detached intellect used to handling disasters.

So finally Sopwith came to the verge of facing the unpalatable truth: that he was neither very bright, nor very nice.

His sole talent, he understood with a bubble of revulsion rising from his digestive tract, was a small curious capacity for bloodletting in front of a camera.

"Camera," he moaned, seizing the least ruinous of these dribbles of association. "Exactly. Grab them by the throat and shake them. Hard-hitting research. Why isn't The Gnome here to tell me what to do?"

He sat up so hard he cracked his head on the Porsche's low hood. The effect of the blow, together with the throbbing from his bruised cheek, combined the two principal comic-book conventions of his childhood—the pointy stars of pain, and the brilliant illuminated light bulb of inspiration.

Head ringing, making grunting sounds like an animal gnawing off its foot to escape a trap, he twisted the ignition, backed the vehicle into Clowes Street with some damage to the gears, and left a foul cloud of scorched rubber and fuel fractions behind to mar the fragrant South Yarra air.

It took slightly longer than he'd anticipated.

The man at the Registry office had gone home to his forsaken Sunday night family, but not, thank Christ, without leaving the documents pinned in an envelope to the main door of the building. Sopwith snatched them down, leafed feverishly, ran to the car.

"There's the seaman's mission."

"Yes," he panted. "Of course. Port Melbourne."

It was not the wedding of the year.

There were no merry bells.

No confetti fell like unseasonable snow in summer.

Not one giggling bridesmaid selected from a proud team of nieces and bosom friends caught the bride's flung bouquet. In fact, Sopwith had overlooked flowers entirely.

For witnesses he'd collared a pair of half-whacked bilge-scrubbers with bleary eyes and stubbled chins who agreed to sign their names in exchange for a bottle of Grange Hermitage that Sopwith had been saving for a special occasion, though one grumbled and wished for a flagon of port instead.

"You've lost your mind," said the new Mrs. Hammil as he bundled her into his sports coupe. "Who'd ever have dreamed Sopwith Hammil would make such a resolute swain?"

"You said yes, didn't you?" Sopwith mumbled ungraciously, running a red light.

"How could I have said no, after you broke the poor man's toe in your rush along the aisle to reach me?"

"I didn't mean to step on his toe, Mariette. But I couldn't wait until the play finished." He crashed the car into top gear and blazed along St. Kilda Road toward his Collins Street bachelor unit.

Bachelor no longer, he reminded himself with a rush of relief.

The dash clock gave him eleven minutes to beat the insect into his living room.

"Darling," his wife said, an edge to her voice, "must you rush everywhere? We haven't even paused for a proper kiss. Or," she murmured, smiling slyly, "are you so anxious to have me in your bed?"

"Trust me, Gno—Mariette." Sopwith swerved at high speed to avoid a busload of nuns. "Explain everything when we get home. My love," he added carefully.

He bounded up the first four flights, not willing to wait for the lift, dragging his wife at the end of his arm. Man, woman, and elevator coincided at the fourth level, and they rose together smoothly to the tenth floor.

The living room was empty.

Face bloody with exertion, heart rattling with relief, Sopwith sat Mariette Hammil, nee Planck, in his hand-stitched leather sofa and made them both a strong drink.

She looked around with a measure of admiration. "I've never been here before," she said. "It's not bad, though I deplore that tacky bar."

"The bar came with me from my last place. The rest is interior decoration," Sopwith said with a trace of pique.

Still, what did it matter? Everything would be left behind, and they could forge fresh tastes in common in an era where undoubtedly all the furniture would be made of sheer energy fields or something.

His wife put aside her full glass. "You don't want to go to bed straightaway?"

"Mariette, drink your drink and listen to what I tell you," Sopwith said. "You're going to see something in a moment that will be so terrifying that I probably should have given you a tranquillizer as well."

"Go on," Mariette said, and you could tell she'd have nudged him in the ribs if she hadn't been sitting down in a squishy sofa on the other side of the room. "I've been around a bit."

"No, no." Sopwith snatched at his head in an Arabic gesture of frustration. "Look, the fact is, I was visited earlier tonight by a creature from—"

In the center of the room the air curdled, bubbled, popped, and emitted Moog noises.

The insectoid solidified, tucked neatly into a meter-high surgical boot.

It bowed from the waist toward Mariette.

"Ah, Mr. Hammil. I see you have brought your mate with you." It gestured in Sopwith's direction with a thing like a fly's hairy leg if a fly were two meters tall.

"That's my *wife* you're talking to, damn it," Sopwith said, offended. *"I'm standing over here."*

"Oh yes." It swung clumsily about, made an apologetic bow. "One is so accustomed to bodily metamorphosis, one finds difficulty in telling you somatically rigid primitives apar—"

Mariette, while the thing was distracted by her husband, bounded from the sofa and clamped her hands around its ghastly hairy right wrist.

With a shriek, it tried to pull free.

"Hey—" Sopwith cried. "You can't touch it, it isn't actually—"

"Release me, you imbecile," it snarled at Mariette. "You're pulling me into the timeflow. You'll jam me here in the past."

"Kaluza-Klein energy skein," Mariette panted, her plain little face shining with triumph. "I knew I'd force a paradox sooner or later and bring you back here after me. Time Patrol, eh? What century?"

"What are you babbling about, woman? 'Time Patrol'?" The insectoid was scandalized. "How tawdry. I am a political figure of some note, madame, not a custodial functionary. Unhand me, I say!"

Mariette tightened her grip until the being yelped.

"What century?" she insisted.

Sopwith gaped. This person was steely and definite, hard and powerful, and he decided he had never seen her before in his life.

What a wonderful institution marriage is, he told himself, agog. It matures the character while rewarding the baser impulses.

"The forty-seventh, if you must know. And you?"

"None of your business, buster. Are you telling me you haven't been sent to intercept me?"

"My dear woman, never until this moment have I even *conceived* that a creature such as yourself might exist in this primitive era. Are you truly the male's spouse?"

"We've just contracted a form of marriage," Mariette admitted, "though it is yet to be consummated. I admit I was a little puzzled by Sopwith's sudden enthusiasm, but then I'm still finding my emotional bearings in this barbarous century. It's all your doing, then?"

"You're hurting my leg," the insectoid said wetly. "There's no point blaming me for any of this. I just work here. I thought I was doing you both a favor."

Moog bleatings and hummings and arpeggios got louder as the thing made this declaration, and started hurting everyone's eardrums.

"Now what are you doing? There's an illicit force field in this room! Turn it off!"

The rasping noise rose and rose and somehow it seemed that the walls flickered and spun with moiré interference patterns that baffled the eye and made you feel horribly dizzy and—

Joe Wagner's Striped Hole, drawn to Mariette's Hyperspatial implants as irresistibly as a silkworm moth to the heavenly tang of bombykol, crashed backwards across less than a day of time and southwards a thousand kilometers of space, burst like spherical lightning or a nuclear explosion in the first microsecond of fireball or a very, very hot radiating piece of blue-vein cheese into the air above Mariette's frizzy red hair.

Tremendous sparks jumped between the Hole and her bared, ecstatic teeth.

Sobbing with joy, she released the insectoid's hairy manipulator.

Against all expectations, the alien from the forty-seventh century did not instantly activate its controls and zot away into the awful gulfs of futurity, because though it was a rather pinched, self-righteous, and bureaucratic person, it had by this point built up sufficient sense of involvement in the ongoing situation and its concomitant transactional analyses to wonder just what the hell was going on and how it would all turn out.

Sopwith staggered back until a protruding portion of his kitschy bar struck him painfully in the sacroiliac.

Lightning played like blue kittens up and down Mariette's arms.

Saint Elmo's Fire settled on her eyeballs.

Something sizzled and spat and smelled like frying insulation.

Mariette held the Striped Hole in her left hand and prodded at its superstrings with her right, teasing out the spare end.

The apartment's fire alarms started to ring, and the damaged Bang & Olufsen sound system went into spasms, settling at last, to Sopwith's horror, on the Easy Listening AM station which it played at full volume under considerable distortion due to the torrential electromagnetic fields smashing through the room.

"Grab my leg," Mariette yelled, sitting down hard on the carpet and bracing herself against the sofa.

Sopwith stared at her, clutching his head.

"Grab my right foot, you half-witted imbecile," Mariette screamed. "Soppy, I'm sorry. I know you're frightened. It's all right. Come on, just do me a little favor and pull on my right leg, there's a good boy."

The sprinklers came on, drenching the carpet, the sound system, the leather-bound books in their small carved case.

Sopwith crept forward through the pyrotechnics and took Mariette's right clubbed boot in his nerveless fingers.

He pulled.

Her boot stuck, resisting his efforts.

"Harder. Put your back into it."

There was a sharp shearing sound as the Hyperspatial implant gave up the ghost. Sopwith felt the boot come free. He staggered backwards, still pulling.

He continued to pull for some time after the boot should have been off.

He started to scream and gibber.

"Your leg's coming off," he shrieked. "Oh my God, Mariette, I've pulled your leg off."

But it hadn't come off, it had just got longer and longer and more absurd, sticking out like a stocking ad in some classy fashion magazine or an illustration of body tone in an aerobics glossy. The other leg sat next to it stumpily.

"Do the left one now."

"You want me to pull your other leg off," Sopwith babbled incredulously.

"Do it," Mariette said in a voice like two glaciers passing on a dark night, "or I'll have this thing over here *eat your head.*"

"I say," the insectoid began, but Sopwith had lurched forward convulsively and with one back-straining heave released Hsia Shan-yun's left leg.

She rose in at least some of her glory and threw back her head, yelling her triumph in rather the way Johnny Weissmuller did after he'd mangled something three times his size in the jungle.

The fire flaring at her eyes branched, ran across her scalp, burned off the frizzy rubbish and set free her wild black hair so it whirled like a drunken night as she tossed her head. Her eyes were huge and slashed and green as glowing jade, and something caught the flesh of her mean little mouth and tore, tore away the invisible bandages, and her wonderful lips opened wide onto teeth meant for a carnivore.

The alien from the future watched this transformation with pleasure.

"Excellent. Most tastefully done. I think the arms remain a little underconceptualized, though, and the torso now seems a trifle *mince*, no?"

Shan-yun laughed balefully, throwing off her demure jacket and neat little silk blouse and drawing her arms out of their sockets, stretching the flesh and muscle like soft toffee, and then, holding the hissing Striped Hole tightly between her knees, delicately tugged out each finger to its decent length, squeezing and kneading and palping the poor crushed things back to life.

"Turn the extinguisher system off, Sopwith," she said soothingly.

The floor was soaked. People should have been pounding at the door of the apartment, but some bubble of local energy centered on the Striped Hole seemed to hold the room in a kind of secluded limbo. Sobbing, Sopwith stumbled to the panel that controlled his alarms and protective devices and switched everything but the sound system off.

He got back just in time to see Shan-yun unclip her brassiere and pry open her chest.

The sight unhinged him.

"I don't want to go anymore," he told the alien, crouching beside its boot.

"What?"

"Just leave me here to freeze when the sun's turned off. I won't tell anyone."

The alien monster could hardly drag away its admiring gaze, but Sopwith's blithering and pestering finally got its goat.

"Look, I'm afraid that was all a mistake in any case. I only came back tonight to tell y—"

"A *mistake!*" Sopwith screamed. "How could it be a

mistake? How can anyone make a mistake about a thing like the sun going out?''

''Actually,'' the alien said modestly, ''I like to think I played some small part in having the decision rescinded.''

''The Earth's *not* going to freeze?''

''Thankfully, not for some billions of years. You're perfectly safe.''

''The sun?'' Shan-yun said acutely, looking up from her final detailed bodywork. ''You fools were tinkering with the sun?''

''Well, you can't put the blame on me,'' the insectoid told her, aggrieved. ''As I was just telling your husband, my flange of the Solar Energy Conservation Party has had a famous victory and managed to get the ruling—''

''Very likely.'' In the new remodelled Mariette's voice, Sopwith heard the rasping skepticism which, together with the illegal history she'd memorized as a child, had made her so resolute and brilliant a research assistant. ''I don't suppose the engineers just happened to uncover certain intractable technical difficulties at the site?''

Startled, the alien drew back its head, at least insofar as this action was consistent with its lack of a proper neck.

''That information is meant to be restricted under privilege. Speaking of which,'' it said sternly, rallying, ''what are you doing in possession of a Striped Hole? Don't you know that sort of thing can lead to hopeless time loops? We could all be stuck in this dreadful era forever.''

''I should think Soppy's friend O'Flaherty Gribble built it,'' Shan-yun said.

''He's no friend of mine.''

''You can't say I haven't tried,'' Shan said. ''I've steered you in his direction so often I'm surprised you didn't marry *him* instead of me.''

Sopwith looked away in disgust. He was a *man's* man, not a man's *man*.

''You've been interfering with the past!'' the insect cried in horror and accusation. ''Madness! A capital offense!

Are you actually going to stand there and admit giving a twentieth-century human person the secret of Kaluza-Klein Hole plaiting?''

Shan-yun was drifting like a ghost about the living room, squelching in the wet carpet, performing slow, beautiful Tai Chi *katas* to get her freed body back under perfect control.

"Don't be absurd. No, I just nudged Soppy here to get O'Flaherty on the show as often as possible. I knew someone would cotton on eventually and come get me. And here you are.''

"Hmph. For a different reason entirely.''

"No such thing as a coincidence,'' Shan-yun told the insect, sublimely confident. The Hole seethed and glowed like a ball of glowing, knotted neon tubing above her head, moving gracefully with her. "Can't you guess what went wrong with your engineers' projections?''

"Restricted information,'' the alien grumbled.

"Precisely. You don't know.'' She reached above her head and twirled the ball of force. *"This* is what happened—''

And she threw the Striped Ball at the ceiling.

It soared and swelled, light spitting at its boundaries. Like a monstrous dandelion fluffball of radiance, it passed from the room without physically leaving it.

"—into the sun? Getting there *yesterday?''* shouted the insect.

"Bull's-eye,'' Shan said, grinning from ear to ear.

"But how do you expect to get home?''

"Actually,'' said Hsia Shan-yun, seizing the creature's chitinous shoulder with one strong hand and its hairy upper limb with the other, "I was hoping you'd drop me off.'' She bared her teeth. "If you're going my way.''

"Wait, wait,'' cried Sopwith Hammil, standing like a fool in the middle of his drenched room listening to the sounds of Mantovani in the background, "you can't just go off like this! We're married, Mariette. You're my wife, God damn it.''

"My name's Hsia Shan-yun, tooter.'' She started to fade from sight, holding the alien's arm in a hammerlock. "Console yourself with the thought that at least you didn't get sent back into the past to spend the rest of your days with a tribe of *Australopithecus boisei.*''

And she was gone.

Sopwith Hammil wandered in a daze. After a while he changed the station to 3RRR and got a blast of heavy sounds from the Razored Eyeball. He dug out a fat sponge and a plastic bucket and started mopping up his floor.

He found himself on his knees, swaying gently back and forth.

"Australopithecus boisei?'' he said.

He went back to the bar and carefully made himself a Headbanger, then another.

"O'Flaherty Gribble,'' he told himself thickly. "Fool of a man. Must ring him. Tomorrow. Give him a call. Fool of a man. Poor Cyn.''

From somewhere nearby, George Bone looked down on Sopwith and smiled at what he saw. It was the kind of warm, accepting, absolutely trustworthy smile every kid wants from his dad.

DAMIEN BRODERICK is an Australian writer who has produced five science fiction novels since his first book publication, *Sorcerer's World*, in 1970. He has been a leading light in Australian SF publishing with two Ditmar Awards to his credit. *The Dreaming Dragons* was a runner-up for the John W. Campbell Memorial Award on its American publication. His most recent novel, *Transmitters*, revolves around the world of science fiction fans but is not itself science fiction.

Broderick is addicted to polysyllabic wordplay and serious writing. He currently lives in Brunswick, a suburb of Melbourne.

BIO OF A SPACE TYRANT
Piers Anthony

"Brilliant...a thoroughly original thinker and storyteller with a unique ability to posit really *alien* alien life, humanize it, and make it come out alive on the page." *The Los Angeles Times*

A COLOSSAL NEW FIVE VOLUME SPACE THRILLER—
BIO OF A SPACE TYRANT
The Epic Adventures and Galactic Conquests of Hope Hubris

VOLUME I: REFUGEE　　　　84194-0/$3.50 US/$4.50 Can
Hubris and his family embark upon an ill-fated voyage through space, searching for sanctuary, after pirates blast them from their home on Callisto.

VOLUME II: MERCENARY　　　87221-8/$3.50 US/$4.50 Can
Hubris joins the Navy of Jupiter and commands a squadron loyal to the death and sworn to war against the pirate warlords of the Jupiter Ecliptic.

VOLUME III: POLITICIAN　　　89685-0/$3.50 US/$4.50 Can
Fueled by his own fury, Hubris rose to triumph obliterating his enemies and blazing a path of glory across the face of Jupiter. Military legend...people's champion...promising political candidate...he now awoke to find himself the prisoner of a nightmare that knew no past.

THE BEST-SELLING EPIC CONTINUES—
VOLUME IV: EXECUTIVE
89834-9/$3.50 US/$4.50 Can
Destined to become the most hated and feared man of an era, Hope would assume an alternate identify to fulfill his dreams ...and plunge headlong into madness.

VOLUME V: STATESMAN
89835-7/$3.50 US/$4.95 Can
the climactic conclusion of Hubris' epic adventures:

AVON Paperbacks